First Love Paperback Copyright © 2018 Lorhainne Ekelund
Editor: Talia Leduc

All rights reserved.
ISBN-13: 978-1998775507

Give feedback on the book at:
lorhainneeckhart@hotmail.com

Twitter: @LEckhart
Facebook: AuthorLorhainneEckhart

Printed in the U.S.A

First Love

THE FRIESSENS
BOOK SIX

LORHAINNE ECKHART

**Everyone said they were too young to fall
in love**

Katy and Steven have planned out their happily ever after: marriage, family, and a place of their own. A simple life in a small town with big dreams, just like Katy's parents, Brad and Emily.

However, life's hardships soon threaten the future Steven and Katy have planned together.

CHAPTER
One

Yellow was Katy's favorite color, and having the sun stream in the bedroom window, casting light over the white walls and the vivid yellow print of her duvet first thing in the morning, brought a smile to her face. She stretched and, like every morning, could hear voices outside on the ranch, clatter downstairs from her mom cooking, and then the familiar call of "Katy, Becky, time to get up!" Trevor, her older brother, who had autism, would already be up, of course, as he was every morning.

Her mom was Emily Friessen, formerly Nelson, and Katy still carried her other dad's name—not that Brad wasn't her dad. Technically, he was her stepdad, and he had become her legal guardian, taking care of the question of who was responsible for her if something happened to Emily. Her name now told the story: Katy Nelson-Friessen. Brad would always be the father who had raised her, had been there for her through all the good, the bad, and the everyday events of life. He was the father she needed, trusted, looked up to, the one she went to for everything.

Her real dad lived up in Olympia, and she saw him as often as she could, but he just stayed in touch and played a background role in her life. He was not the type who, when push came to shove, would stand and fight for her or be the watchdog at her door. That was Brad. No, Katy's birth father, Bob Nelson, wasn't made that way. He loved her, but he had a life elsewhere and didn't have an alpha bone in his body. Maybe that should have bothered her more, but it didn't. He was just her dad.

Katy had a home, a family, parents she loved and looked up to, a baby brother just learning to walk, a sister who annoyed her at times, and a stepbrother who was a few years older. She and Trevor were close. He counted on her, and she looked out for him. Helping him was second nature. Tomorrow she would be eighteen, graduating grade twelve in two weeks, and she was in love with Steven Bennett.

She knew people didn't take their commitment seriously and maybe considered them too young to understand what love was, but what they needed to understand was that Steven was her first love, her true love, her only love. Her cell phone buzzed from where she'd tucked it under her pillow. She didn't need to look to know who was calling, but his handsome face with dimples flashed on the screen.

"Hi," she said. She always felt her insides turn to mush at the sound of Steven's voice.

"Have you told your parents yet?" His deep voice had her wanting to wrap her arms a little tighter around her stomach, dreamily wishing he was there and that she could touch him. She loved the feel of him, his touch, his kiss, just being with him. She ached when he was gone.

"No. I will today, I promise," she said, glancing at her door, hearing the footsteps and fearing time was almost up.

"I should be there with you."

"Katy, I called you already…" Emily opened the door, gesturing at her because she had the phone stuck to her ear again. "Hang it up already. You need to be ready for school. You're not even dressed."

"Steven, I've got to go."

"Love you," he said, and she couldn't smother the big grin that swept across her face.

"I love you, too."

Her mom stepped into the bedroom. Her baby brother, Jack, was resting on her hip in just a diaper and T-shirt. His thick dark hair, unusual for a baby, was sticking straight up. He had Brad's expression, her mom's eyes, and a strong personality. She'd heard her mom say many times that Jack was stubborn and difficult just like the Friessen men.

She dropped her phone on the bed as she got up, her pale green nightgown riding higher as she slipped from bed. "Mom, can I get dressed?" she said, wondering about the way Emily was watching her, her expression. Katy knew her mom was wondering whether she was keeping something from her. She'd seen it a hundred times before as if her mom was trying to yank her back to being the little girl who had shared everything.

"So what's going on?" Emily said. "Steven's calling again, and so early." Her mom was making a face, and then something in her expression, around her eyes, seemed concerned. "I know we've talked about this love thing, how you think you and Steven are—"

"Oh my God, Mom, would you stop? We are in love," she snapped, interrupting Emily before she could tell her one more time how to feel, how it was impossible for someone almost eighteen to understand grownup love, how it was just infatuation. It hurt the way her mother made her feel she didn't know her own mind. Even Brad had stepped in a few times and warned Emily to stop.

"Watch your mouth, Katy." Emily stepped back, frowning again, looking to the window. "Just hurry and get dressed or you're going to miss the bus, and I don't have time to drive you today." She started out the door but stopped, her hand on the doorknob as she faced Katy again.

"You know, Mom, I could drive myself—should drive myself. I don't understand why you have to treat me like a child. The few times you've let me get behind the wheel, it's a wonder I know how to drive at all." She'd even asked her dad if she could have a car, but he'd said no, as he'd gotten rid of all the old vehi-cles parked around the house except for her mom's minivan and his brand-new truck, one her mom didn't drive very often.

"You can when you have a car of your own—which you need a job to pay for. Oh, and to get a good job you need to have an education, so get dressed, hurry up, and maybe focus more on school today and less on Steven."

She just had to say it again, and now Katy couldn't help worrying about what else her mom was going to ram down her throat about how she thought she should feel or act. She didn't talk this way to Becky or Trevor, and Katy was beginning to resent her mom's interference more and more.

Maybe it was her growing frown, as she could feel her radiant good mood heading right into the trash, that had her mom sighing and backing out. "Never mind. Just get dressed," Emily said, and she closed the door behind her.

Katy couldn't help reaching for the phone again and dialing before she heard a tap on the door. It opened again.

"Oh, yeah, and no more phone tucked under your pillow, Katy. Your room is for sleeping, not talking on your cell phone. I want to see it downstairs from now on, plugged in with ours, or no more phone. Understand?"

Katy dumped the phone on the bed again, and this time when the door closed she went over and pressed the lock in the center of the brass handle. She leaned against the door and listened to her mom in the hallway, now on to Becky, nagging her about something she was wearing. Good! Katy smiled as she reached for her phone to call Steven again as she searched her closet for something to wear.

CHAPTER

Two

Brad was an extremely handsome man. Even though he wasn't Katy's real father, he was the one she looked to for everything. Seeing her mom and how she responded to him, Katy knew he could get Emily to do anything. He was the only man who could reason with her mom, soften her, and get her to see things his way.

She was almost embarrassed to tell her friends how her parents behaved, considering the number of times she'd walked into the kitchen or living room or barn to find her parents locked together, deep in a kiss filled with so much heat and passion that she'd finally learned to clear her throat just to announce she was there.

"G-rated house, Mom, Dad," she said that morning as she watched her dad leaning down to her mom, his lips on hers as he held Jack. Emily rested her hand on Brad's cheek, and he was fresh from the barn after early morning chores. He appeared ready for the day, the same as every morning, dressed in faded jeans and a blue shirt. He was so tall and strong, a man who let Katy know she'd never have to worry about anything. It wasn't something he'd said; it was everything he did.

"Hey, you. Your mom said she caught you on your phone this morning, talking instead of getting ready. Think we talked about this already." Brad didn't move from where he lingered by Emily.

"You missed the bus, Katy," her mom added as she lifted a frypan from the stove and rested it in the sink. "Is that what you're wearing today?"

Of course it was. Katy loved the low dip of the white tee, which showed her cleavage, just a hint but enough that she knew Steven would appreciate it. She'd opted for a jean skirt today. It was decent, barely about a hand's length from her knee. She remembered well the new dress code the school had imposed, mainly because of the truly indecent cutoffs the popular girls wore to show off the edge of their curvy bottoms. Katy would never dare, mainly because her parents would never let her out of the house dressed that way. "Something wrong with what I'm wearing?" she asked, wondering whether her mom would make her change her top.

Instead Emily sighed. "Guess not." She looked to Brad, who Katy could tell was deciding.

She half expected her dad to tell her to go change, but he took in her mom again before passing Jack to her. "I'll drive you," he said, reaching into his pocket and pulling out a set of keys.

Emily handed Katy an apple from a bowl on the table. "Eat this," she said, giving Katy a look that had her rolling her eyes. She felt a hand rest on her shoulder.

"Katy, don't do that disrespectful crap anymore," Brad said. "Let's go. Got everything?" He started to the door, his cowboy boots scraping on the floor, keys jingling in his hands. "Em, you need anything in town since I'm there?"

"No, but I'm going out with Candy later if you can watch Jack while I'm gone for a few hours."

Her dad just lifted his hand and winked at Emily as Katy took a bite of the apple she didn't have an appetite for. She chewed to appease her mom, not wanting to hear about how she needed to eat breakfast before school. Then she was at the door, lifting her already stuffed deep purple backpack, knowing her mom had already packed her lunch for her. Maybe she should insist she stop?

Brad was waiting for her at the bottom of the steps, and he smiled. She wondered for a moment, by the expression on his face, whether he too wanted to say something, so she took another bite of her apple, feeling the weight of the backpack with all her unfinished homework, books, and lunch tucked inside.

"How's Steven?" Brad asked as he started to the truck and opened the passenger door for Katy. She slid in.

"He's good. Oh, Dad, I want to talk to you and mom about something tonight," she added.

Of course Brad raised an eyebrow, just taking her

in without saying a word. Then he gestured to her seatbelt. "Fasten up," he said before closing her door.

He went around to his side, pulled open the door, and slid behind the wheel. It wasn't like her dad not to say anything, and he seemed to be considering something as he backed up and pulled down the driveway to the highway. "Got a call last night from your teacher. Was wondering if you forgot to mention something to us."

The way he'd said it had Katy scrambling, trying to figure out which teacher had called. Oh, crap, this wasn't good. She could feel her dad glance over.

"If you're trying to figure out what to say or whether to lie, think again. Told you not to keep things from us. It may be your birthday tomorrow, Katy, but I won't hesitate to ground you."

"I'm at a loss of what to say. You know Mrs. Moore is old and cranky. I swear I did my best on that English report, but she failed me. I'm sorry, but—"

Brad was shaking his head. "Not Mrs. Moore, Katy, but that's good to know you're failing English, too. Just what exactly are you doing in school?"

What could she say? School was just that, a place to go during the day, with nothing that inspired her. No, Steven was good in school. He'd focused, applied himself, and he'd still had time for Katy before graduating the previous year. She shrugged. "It's just school, Dad. I mean, how am I going to use any of the stuff they're teaching, anyway?"

She could hear the scrape of his whiskers as he rubbed his hand across his chin. "Katy, I know you've told us you don't want to go to college. You're graduating in a few weeks, but the call we got from your history teacher, you know, the one who's also your counsellor, was unsettling."

She wanted to wince. Mr. Rumpel had called her in a couple times, sitting her down in his office and asking about her plans for after graduation. He'd been frank, even tried to give her the tough love thing about dead-end jobs and what it meant to have no education.

"He said he's concerned because your grades from your final aren't going to give you enough to graduate. The only course that's passable is math, and barely, according to Mr. Rumpel. Katy, this isn't a joke. A high school diploma isn't just something that's nice to have. It's necessary."

"Fine, I get it, Dad. I'll make it up, whatever I need to do, like night classes next year."

"Well, that's the thing, Katy. You need to pull it together. Your mom and I had no idea it was this bad at school, and your teacher said it was just this last semester, as if you've decided you're done. I remember clearly that we asked you how school was going, your classes, homework, exams, everything… and you told us it was good. I can't believe your teacher is only letting us know now, when it's too late to do something this year."

Katy just sat in silence, not wanting to admit that she'd let her studies go since deciding she was done with school, just counting the days until it was over.

Brad pulled into the parking lot at the high school and parked.

"Dad, what are you doing?" Katy said. He usually dropped her off at the front doors, never parked and turned off his truck and got out, as he was doing now. She opened her door and stepped down to where her dad was waiting. He gestured toward the school.

"What I'm doing, Katy, is walking you in. Oh, and did I mention my meeting with Mr. Rumpel this morning?"

The way he said it made Katy feel as if the ground had fallen out beneath her. Of course he hadn't mentioned it, and she knew that had been intentional.

"Hmm, guess I forgot," Brad said. He rested his hand on her shoulder as they walked side by side to the front doors of the school, where her friends and the other teens were hanging out, just as the bell rang and the doors flew open. Great. Now she really did feel as if she were twelve years old.

Three

"So how did it go at school?" Emily had brushed her brown hair until it hung in soft waves down her back. She was wearing a plaid brown western shirt that was tapered at the waist and showed off her slim figure, lowrider jeans, and a leather belt with pink stones on the buckle. She had also slipped on small gold hoops, and as she looked up to Brad with her soft blue eyes, he could see the woman he loved.

She insisted on having her own time now, something she hadn't done when the other kids were young. Maybe it was their age now, at almost fifty, that made Emily not want to revert back to being a young mother whose entire focus was her children and husband—not that she didn't focus on them now. It was just that with the kids being older and Emily discovering herself pregnant with Jack just when she had her freedom back, it was the one thing she wouldn't give up. Brad couldn't deny her time to herself with Candy, her sister-in-law, since having a baby at their age had been a surprise that had tested their relationship.

Brad glanced to the stairs, taking in the quiet in the house. "Jack asleep?" He was planning on catching up on some paperwork while Emily was out. He shared more of the day-to-day caregiving of Jack than he had of any of the other kids, and he enjoyed those small moments of peace.

"Yeah, just, after he rearranged all the pots and pans, the containers. Time to baby proof the cupboards again." She handed Brad the baby monitor as she slipped her socked feet into half boots that came up to her ankles. Then she stood up, rested her hand on his cheek, and kissed him. She frowned as she pulled back. "You didn't answer me about school, about the call we got."

This was the first time he'd seen Emily pull back and allow him to talk to the school, the teachers, without her. Maybe she was easing up a bit. It was a good thing.

"Oh, let's see. Katy should be graduating in two weeks, but she hasn't actually graduated high school because she's failed just about every subject except math, which, you'll be happy to know, she passed by the skin of her teeth. Apparently the grades slipping is something that's only happened this past semester. She slapped together her last exams and final reports as an afterthought, and all that time she's been spending in her room, apparently studying, I can guarantee you she was goofing off and probably talking to Steven."

Brad continued. "Katy seems to think it's no big deal, that she just needs to take a few classes at night school in the fall, but the problem is, Em, we've done everything for her. She's never really had a job except here on the ranch, helping out, doing chores. She doesn't seem to have a grasp on what she needs to do to survive out there. The only job she'd be able to get is some minimum-wage job in a fast-food restaurant."

Emily opened her mouth, her expression letting Brad know she had a few choice things to say to her daughter. Then she sighed, resting her hand on his arm. "I guess we should sit her down, talk to her. With her birthday tomorrow, eighteen, I just wanted it to be special, and now this."

Brad slipped his hand around her arm. "We'll talk to her tonight, and her birthday will be special. It's just that she's idealistic, doesn't see the bad part of this world. Maybe we've sheltered her too much."

"I don't know, Brad. She's lucky she's never had to worry, knowing you were there watching her back. I can't fault that. Maybe this is on me for needing her here, too, helping out around here. I've sheltered her so much I wonder if she'd know how to stand on her own two feet."

A vehicle pulled up outside. Brad didn't need to look to know it was Candy, his brother's wife, whom Emily was closer to than any two sisters could be. "Have fun with Candy," he said as she kissed him again, then reached for her purse and went out the door.

Just as the taillights of Candy's car disappeared onto the highway, a light blue Cavalier pulled in. It was Steven, Katy's boyfriend, who had graduated the previous year and was now enrolled in a trade school to be an electrician. He was now apprenticing with a local company, which, in Brad's opinion, was a smart choice.

He pushed open the screen door and stepped out as Steven parked and climbed out, wearing dark blue pants and a shirt, the company uniform. His dark hair was clipped short. He was tall and lanky for a young man of nineteen. Despite the recent issues with Katy, Brad had to admit he rather liked Steven's ideals.

"Hi, Mr. Friessen," Steven said. "Was wondering if I could have a moment to speak with you."

He was polite, too, another trait Brad liked, especially considering he hadn't been too inclined to like any young man coming around to date his daughters. However, Steven and Katy had been dating for the past three years, and Brad realized this wasn't just a light friendship.

"Sure you can. Everything all right?" he asked, taking in the young man, who stopped at the bottom of the stairs and jammed his hands in his pockets before pulling them out again and rubbing them together. It was a motion Brad recognized, that of a boy not quite sure of something. He was nervous.

"Well, sir, I know Katy wanted to talk to you

herself. In fact, I insisted she did, but I really feel I should be talking with you, you know, man to man."

Brad tried not to laugh, and it took everything in him not to smile in amusement. The kid had no idea what it was to be a man, being so young, but he had confidence and wasn't scared of approaching Brad—another point in the kid's favor. Damn, Brad didn't have to like it, though.

He said nothing, just stood there waiting for Steven to talk. He crossed his arms, and Steven flushed. Of course he was making him nervous. Good!

"Not easy coming here," Steven said. He smiled nervously, and Brad was starting to wonder what was going on.

"Spit it out. Make it painless and get to the point," he finally said.

"You're right." Steven sucked in a breath. "I wanted to ask your permission to marry Katy."

Brad breathed in his nose and then out, feeling his arms tighten. Yes, he remembered the boy mentioning just the previous year that he planned to marry Katy, so now he was asking. Brad had hoped this day would never come.

"August 18, sir, a summer wedding."

Okay, way too soon and not what he'd expected. This wasn't going to happen.

He shook his head and then pushed away from the post, taking in the wide steps, the white stain beginning to peel and chip again. He needed to strip it back and restain before the fall. He rested his hands on his hips and then lowered them to his sides as he went down the steps. Steven took a step back, maybe because Brad was now so close in his face that he could feel his heat. He could see how scared the boy was, a young man who had a light shadow on his chin from the spots that grew hair. He hadn't shaved today.

"Let me get this straight," Brad said. "You're nineteen, just. You're working as an electrical apprentice making, what, fifteen, twenty thousand a year?"

"Twenty-four, sir," Steven added as if it made any difference. It was still a poverty wage that would pay for nothing.

"Okay, twenty-four thousand just as an apprentice. You live with your parents—"

"I rented my own place in town last week. It's a small one bedroom, but it's mine. I move in in three days," he said, interrupting Brad, which didn't make him happy in the least.

"Okay, and you want to get married, from my count, in under two months?" Even as he said it, he couldn't help the awful feeling that came over him. He wondered whether he could keep himself from wrapping his hands around the kid's throat and squeezing or simply kick his ass right off the property before the feeling went from bad to worse. "You get Katy pregnant?" he snarled.

Maybe it was the dark look Brad leveled his way that had Steven holding his hands up, his expression panicked. "No, no, nothing like that, sir. Oh, man, I'm really messing this up. No, Katy and I love each other. Truly, we do. We've talked about this, and this is what we want, what we planned."

Brad had to remind himself to breathe, to not act but take a minute before speaking. He glanced to the ground and his booted foot, then took in Steven still there before him, sweating but standing his ground. "Marriage is a big step, son, and something no one should go into lightly. Take some time. You and Katy have lots. You're young, and in a few years, after you've established yourself and can support yourself and a family, then we'll talk." He reached out and rested his hand on Steven's shoulder, squeezing just a bit to get his point across so the kid would fall in line with his thinking.

But Steven was shaking his head. Stubbornness was all Brad saw there. "No, sir, I appreciate what you're saying, but Katy and I have decided. We've planned our future out. We have dreams, one of which is to be together, to be married. So, again, sir, I came here out of respect for you and Mrs. Friessen and Katy. I may be young, and maybe we don't know everything yet, but we're not scared to try. I'm not scared, and I'm ready. Katy's ready."

Brad didn't know what to say. Steven's cell phone rang, and he looked to Brad as if needing his permission to answer it. Brad needed a second to figure out how to yell and threaten this young man, so he gestured and stepped back as Steven answered. How could he convince two kids without a clue of the heartache life could toss their way that sometimes it was best to take a minute and look both ways instead of jumping into the middle of a busy freeway? Brad could see the impending disaster coming their way, and it made him angry that Steven wasn't hearing him. Brad felt as if he had no control, as if there wasn't a damn thing he could do to stop it, and not being able to control a situation that affected his family, his children, worried him.

"That was my boss. Sorry, Mr. Friessen. I have to get back to work." Steven had his hands shoved in his pockets now, but he pulled one out and stuck it forward, a gesture Brad took in. He liked Steven as much as he could any boy pawing at his daughter. After a few seconds, maybe to put the kid out of his misery, he accepted the boy's hand and shook, noting the firm grip in someone so young. He patted the boy's shoulder, maybe harder than he should have, and watched as he left, driving a little fast, the way young men did, down the driveway.

Brad stood there, considering his options: locking Katy away, sitting both Katy and Steven down for a talk on some harsh life lessons, or outright forbidding this marriage. He was dreading how Emily was going to take this. Considering how she'd behaved while pregnant with Jack and the rift she'd almost created in her relationship with Katy then, he didn't think she'd take it well at all, but he didn't have a second to consider it, as he heard a babble and then a cry from Jack as he woke from his nap.

Four

Steven needed to talk to Katy, but every time he went to say something to her, his throat closed up. He had seen her twice since showing up at her parents' house and asking, in a manner of speaking, for her hand in marriage from Brad. Despite the fact that the entire show of respect, standing in front of a man he knew could hurt him with little effort, had practically had him crapping his pants, it had turned out nothing as he'd imagined.

Steven respected Brad Friessen. He was a man he looked up to and considered a role model, but standing in front of him with his hat in hand, Steven had seen the moment Brad had considered sending him on his way. He hadn't said he couldn't marry Katy, but he had said they should wait. The fact was, though, that he didn't want to wait, and neither did Katy, This was their dream, their future, and although having her father's blessing—correction, her stepfather's blessing—would have been nice, it wasn't necessary.

He drove out to the ranch with a gold-wrapped box on the passenger seat for Katy, her birthday present, and pulled in beside an SUV, knowing more of her family would be there. He knew one would be Neil, Brad's brother, a man he was a little nervous of, too, along with Candy and their kids, Cat and Michael. To make matters worse, both Brad and Neil were on the porch with beers in hand, chatting, as Steven made his way over to the house.

He knew he was presentable. He'd gone home after work, showered, and changed in the room he'd grown up in. His parents had been at the restaurant, working as they did every night, and he had taken care to dress in newer blue jeans, then pulled on a dark blue dress shirt, his heavy belt with a thick buckle of a horse and rider, and his new work boots.

"Hey, Mr. Friessen." He lifted his hand, for the first time feeling as if he might not be welcome.

"Steven, Katy's been wondering when you were coming." Brad rested his hand on the porch pillar. He smiled, but not the way he normally did. It was forced, tense. Steven glanced over to Neil. The man was gripping his beer, watching Steven in a way that told him Brad had shared his news. Great.

"Steven, you're here!" Katy was out the door, squealing, her long blond hair hanging loose down her back, stopping just above her waist. She was radiant, and her smile could lift him from a shitty day where nothing had gone right to feeling that everything, in that moment, was fantastic. She was down the stairs, wearing a yellow sundress, and she leaped off the last step into his arms. He caught her and all her slimness, holding the small gift box in his one hand, her in the other.

She kissed him, and Steven could feel her dad and uncle watching. He heard one of them clear his throat, and he tried to unlock Katy's arms from around his neck, but her tongue was in his mouth, wrapped to his. This wasn't good. In all her excitement, she could have him doing something that would likely have her dad yanking him away and hurting him. *Down, boy!* he yelled at himself. "Whoa, Katy, your dad's watching us," he said. Then he heard the door squeak again, and this time Katy's mom, Emily, stepped out. He set her down, although she was still plastered against him as if she were a second skin.

"How are you this evening, Mrs. Friessen?" he asked, going through his repertoire of polite banter to break the tension he could feel coming his way.

"Fine, Steven. Good of you to come to Katy's birthday dinner tonight," Emily said, holding a dish-towel, the sound of kids coming from inside the house. "Brad, can you lift that roaster of ribs from the oven? It's too heavy," Emily added.

Just then, Katy noticed the box he was holding. "For me?" She had the perfect smile, and when she was happy she was almost ten feet off the ground. It was infectious.

"Yes, for later," he said.

She shook the box, which fit in the palm of her

hand, pulling her lip between her teeth. "Why wait?" she asked. She was like a little kid as she stepped back, glowing, and went to unwrap the box.

"Katy." He reached for the gift, but she stepped back again and skipped around him as if this were a game. She pulled at the tape, and he reached for her, putting his hand around her waist and lifting her again. He kissed her to distract her, which hadn't been such a great idea, he realized, when he caught Neil watching, appearing uncomfortable and ready, it seemed, to step in and separate them. But at least he now had the gift, as Katy had both hands on him, around his waist.

"Hey, let's go for a walk," she whispered. "Uncle Neil, can you tell Mom and Dad that Steven and I are just going for a walk? We'll be back soon," she called out, reaching for Steven's hand.

Neil waved to them, his expression somewhere between amusement and relief. Steven wasn't a hundred percent sure which—or if it was something entirely different. "Don't be long or go sneaking off to fool around, either. Dinner's almost ready," Neil shouted back, leaning on the rail, his beer dangling from his fingers.

Katy had wanted nothing more than to slip away someplace quiet where she could be alone with Steven, but as soon as they'd rounded the side of the house, his gift for her tucked in his pocket, her dad had opened the back door and whistled the way he did, two fingers in his mouth, so anyone on the next property could have heard.

"Katy, dinner! You and Steven come in and get washed up," he called to her and waited at the door, his hand resting on the screen as if not trusting her to come in.

"They've been keeping me on a short leash lately, it seems, but now that I'm eighteen, an adult, they're going to have to treat me with respect," she said.

Steven didn't say anything as he held her hand and walked toward Brad. He was leading them, and at times he seemed more inclined to go with Brad's way of thinking on things. She wondered how long he'd been like that.

Katy wasn't sure what it was about the way her dad was watching Steven now, but it wasn't with the same welcome lightness he always had before. "I haven't had a chance to talk to Mom and Dad yet," she whispered to Steven, who seemed to tense. The fact was that she'd chickened out the previous night and this morning each time she opened her mouth to say she and Steven were getting married and had set a date. Her mouth wouldn't move. After her birthday, tomorrow would be the day.

Steven stopped at the bottom of the steps, looking up at Brad, still holding Katy's hand, before glancing back at her. "Yeah, but I did. I stopped in yesterday, talked to your dad, and asked for your hand."

Katy couldn't believe what Steven had done. Now she knew why Brad had been watching her the way he had. Why, it seemed every time she had left the room the night before he had been on her about what she was doing, where she was going, and where her phone was. She swallowed, feeling very much like a little girl when, in fact, she was a woman now. She needed to tell her dad just that.

"We'll talk about this later," Brad said. "In the house, both of you. Your mom has gone to a lot of trouble cooking all your favorites and baking a cake for your birthday."

"Mom doesn't know?" She almost wished Brad would have told her and made it easier for her, but that was cowardly. As he shook his head, she felt the flutter in her chest drop to her stomach.

"Let's not start your birthday celebration with

something that's going to upset your mom. We'll talk another day later this week when we can all sit down together."

THE CANDLES WERE LIT on the birthday cake, with thick white frosting and pink lettering reading *Happy 18th Birthday Katy* . Everyone was sitting around the dining room table. Becky and Cat stood behind Katy, and Michael was sitting on Neil's shoulders where he stood behind Candy. Emily had Jack perched on her hip, and everyone was singing to Katy except Trevor, who tapped the table with his hand.

Brad didn't miss how attentive Steven was to Katy. They were glued together, and after having his rose-colored glasses ripped away, Brad could see that it wasn't likely Steven and Katy would come to their senses and realize he was right, that waiting was best. Brad also knew this wasn't something he could afford to take lightly. Everyone was clapping, and after Katy blew out her candles, she kissed Steven, both her hands resting on his cheeks. Brad exchanged a look with Neil, who understood his feelings. He'd shared the details of Steven's visit with his brother shortly after he'd arrived that evening.

"Would you stop all the kissing at the table?" Becky commented, and Katy pulled a face at her sister, who, Brad admitted, could be a nuisance sometimes.

"Let's cut the cake," Brad said before the girls

could start bickering. "I know I can't wait to try what your mom spent all day baking."

"And presents," Katy added as Emily placed a pile of luncheon plates on the table, a handful of dessert forks, and a serrated knife. Katy lifted the candles from the cake, taking a moment to lick the icing from each one. It was then Brad noticed the way Steven watched the motion, and he realized Katy may not be as innocent as he'd expected.

"Cut the cake first and dish it up, and then you can open the presents," Emily said, gesturing to Brad to take Jack. "I want to grab a couple of the gifts I wrapped upstairs."

Brad reached for Jack and watched his wife slip out as Candy said something to Neil. Neil nodded and signed something to Cat, who wasn't wearing her cochlear implant to hear tonight. She signed something back and slipped away, returning a moment later with a box wrapped in pink candy-colored paper, with a huge white bow on top.

Emily followed with a few wrapped gifts and cleared a spot on the table in front of Katy, who cut up the cake and then passed the plates around the table until everyone had a piece. She smiled and giggled as she reached for her first gift. It was these moments Brad loved, seeing her joy and excitement as she tore at the wrapping and exclaimed in excitement over each gift. She hugged Candy and her mom over the dresses and clothes she'd pulled from the boxes, and then there were two small boxes left, one from Steven, the other from Brad and Emily.

His daughter, whom he thought of as his own, glanced at the two boxes, picking up one and then the other. She shook them both and shut her eyes. "Oh, which one next?" She popped open her eyes and grinned brightly as she unwrapped the gold box from Steven and lifted the lid. Her jaw dropped, and her eyes widened.

"Oh my good God, is that an engagement ring?" Emily said as she leaned over her daughter, her hands on the table, her expression that of a woman who'd had the rug ripped out from under her. Why would Steven do this after Brad had made his intentions clear that they were to wait?

Before Brad could do anything like grab Steven by the shirt collar and drag him out to give him a talking to or ask him what the hell he was thinking, the kid slid back his chair, got down on one knee, and said, "Katy Nelson-Friessen, would you marry me?"

Katy didn't know where to look, and her ears were ringing as she vaguely registered the gasps and the quiet that suddenly filled the dining room. Everyone was watching her. Steven was still in front of her on the floor on one knee as she stared at the gold ring with its single small diamond. She didn't need to look up to know her mom was still beside her, and her dad was across the table, holding Jack, his gaze burning into her, into Steven. She looked over to Candy, whose expression was one of disbelief and something else. Neil was shaking his head, and Steven was still there, waiting. This was truly awkward.

She didn't want this to be happening right now. She'd wanted to talk to her mom and dad alone without the entire family standing around, watching, waiting, listening.

"Katy, this is embarrassing. We talked about this," Steven whispered, keeping his voice low, as Katy looked to him. She had to force herself to swallow the lump stuck in her throat. He slipped his hand over hers, lifted the ring from the box, and held it before her finger, and she stared, considered, and hesitated just a second before sliding her tongue over her lips.

"Yes." She squeaked the word out, keeping her eyes on Steven.

Steven smiled as he slipped the ring on her finger. She heard the sharp breath her mom took behind her, which sounded more like a wheeze.

"Katy, you're getting married?" Becky squealed and then jumped in and hugged her. Trevor was frowning, and when Katy glanced up at her mom, it took all the joy that should have been in that moment away. She appeared hurt, and Katy wanted to get up and walk out.

"You're too young to get married," Emily said. "You're eighteen. You haven't even finished school—high school, Katy. You failed your courses, if I can add that little bit." Her mom stepped back, lifted her hands, and then turned to Brad, who was taking everyone in. He only glanced her way a second before turning his heavy gaze on Steven.

"You know what?" Brad said. "We do need to discuss this, but now's not the time."

At least it was out now and she didn't have to worry about telling them. Now she just had to go about convincing them.

"Brad, she just turned eighteen," Emily said. "She's a kid, and she's sitting there with a ring on her finger as if getting married is just the next logical step.

Trevor, Becky, take Cat and Michael with you, and Jack, too. Go watch some TV," Emily added. Her mom sounded mad, hurt, and, although it seemed strange to Katy, betrayed.

She watched her mom reach for Jack and slip him into her younger sister's arms. Evidently, her mom didn't want to wait and was likely to say a few things to her in the next minute.

"Do you two have any idea what getting married is about?" It was Neil who asked as he set Michael down. The boy raced out of the dining room, following his cousins.

"Of course," Steven said as he sat back down in his chair beside Katy, holding her hand again.

Neil was crossing his arms and looked over to Brad, who was unusually quiet. Emily looked fit to be tied again as if still figuring out when she needed to start yelling at Katy. Neil barked a laugh that sounded sarcastic, and Candy, who had been sitting quietly, reached up and touched his arm.

"Neil…" was all she said, but it was effective, because he stopped laughing and instead rested his hands on the back of Candy's seat, standing behind her with a dark look Katy had never seen on his face before.

"Mom and Dad, I'm sorry," she said. "Steven and I have talked about this. It's what we want. We just want a simple life and to eventually have a place of our own. Steven has finished trade school and is apprenticing—"

"I have a promise of full-time employment from

the electrical company come spring, and I rented a sweet little one-bedroom place in town. I'm moving in tomorrow. Katy is—"

"I've talked with Penny Cassidy, who owns that daycare in town," Katy said, interrupting Steven. "She's offered me part-time daycare work this summer and possibly more in the fall."

Her mom had her hand pressed to her mouth. She was pacing small steps back and forth as if she couldn't force herself to stand still. "Are you two crazy? What kind of life is that? I'll tell you what it is. You'll be living hand to mouth, by the sounds of it. You can't understand the hardships of life, of what a relationship is about. Katy, you've never dated anyone else, and you've never lived on your own. You've been here, sheltered, and you've never had to worry about anything. You don't know how to run a household, to live on your own, to balance a life with another person who isn't you—to compromise, and…" Emily lifted her hands and let them fall, looking to Brad as if he would have some words, some divine intervention he could send her way to get Katy and Steven to do as they said.

"Katy." Brad rested his hands on his hips. "You have one more present to open."

She hadn't expected that. She'd forgotten the small blue and white box. She reached for it and pulled open the paper, the excitement and joy of her birthday celebration now dimmed. It contained a small brown box, and she took in the set of keys there and then lifted them out. She glanced over to Brad and then her mom.

"Figured it was time I stopped driving you everywhere," Brad said, unsmiling. "Happy birthday, Katy. We bought you a car."

CHAPTER
Seven

Katy was lying in bed. Jack had finally settled down after crying for a bit because he didn't want to go to sleep, but it was now quiet aside from the sounds of everything on the ranch settling in for the night.

She was eighteen.

She was getting married.

And she now had a car. It was yellow, her favorite color, a Volkswagen Beetle, not brand new but cute as a button. She'd only had time to drive a mile or so down the road before having to turn back with her dad beside her, talking her through the manual transmission. He'd said not one word about her and Steven while sitting in the passenger seat.

Tomorrow, though, would be a different story. First she'd drive herself to school, and then tomorrow night she and Steven had a date with her parents for a sit-down "Let's get tough" talk about the real world, as Brad and Emily had informed her. Neil and Candy had both hugged her before leaving, her uncle pressing a kiss to the top of her head and leveling her with a look that said he would have liked a moment to sit down with her before pulling away with his family.

There was a soft tap on her bedroom door, and then it opened before she could answer. A faint light drifted in, and her mom stood in the doorway. "Are you still awake?" She didn't sound mad anymore, which was good. Katy didn't like when she and her mom were at odds.

"I can't answer you if I'm asleep," she said. Well, that was rude, she realized as soon as it was out of her mouth.

Her mom stepped into the bedroom. "Your dad called to wish you a happy birthday when you were out driving with Brad."

"You didn't tell me," Katy said. She wondered if that had been deliberate. Her mom and real dad never talked at all. Sometimes she wondered if her mom wished he'd just go away.

Emily stepped further into Katy's room, the door open and everything quiet. Her hair was pinned up, and she was wearing her robe, the silky one with rose-buds on it. She must have had a bath. "Your dad wasn't at home and said he'd try you again tomor-row," she said. She was standing at the foot of the bed, her hand resting on the white iron bedframe.

Katy took in her wedding band, the one she always wore, covered in diamonds. It was Brad's ring, and he was a man who made her mom happy. There was love there. It was their relationship that had inspired Katy, something she believed she'd have with Steven.

Katy touched Steven's ring, still on her finger. She should say something to her mom, anything to ease the conflict that seemed to grow between them. She didn't want that. They had always been close. They were still close. "If you're here to talk me out of marrying Steven, please don't," she said, and she watched as her mom glanced to the door and back as if the fight had gone out of her.

She shook her head. "I just don't want to see you make a mistake. Sometimes when you're older and have lived through the hard times, you can see and understand so much more. I just want to protect you and keep everything bad from you. I want you to have choices…"

"Mom, please stop with that, school and me getting some degree as if you think that's the cure for everything." She sat up, the covers dropping to her waist, and she plumped the pillow behind her, then leaned back and pulled her knees up.

"Katy, you just don't know what the world has to offer, and getting married so young…" She stopped, which was good, considering Katy was ready to drop her face in her hands and yell just so she wouldn't hear her mom go on yet again.

"Mom, how many times do I have to tell you until you get it? School isn't for me. I'll get my high school and redo those courses in the fall, get my diploma, but I'm not going to college or university to sit in a bunch of boring classes that don't interest me. I don't have this huge desire for some high-powered career or to be some professional or executive taking on the world. I'm marrying Steven." She pressed her hands to her chest as if that was the only way to get her mom to understand. "I love him, and it's not some infatuation. I thought you would have gotten that by now. I want to marry Steven, to be his wife and make a life together just like you and Dad." How could she not hear her, understand what she was saying?

"I'm just afraid that one day you'll wake up and regret your choices, and I don't want that for you." Her mom sounded so sad.

"But they're my choices, Mom, and, as you believe, my mistakes. Mine. You can't live my life for me. I'm ready, and I want to make my own mistakes, my choices, fix things myself, Mom. I love you and Dad, but you've got to let me breathe. I want to get married, Mom." She didn't say anything else, because her mom wasn't arguing as she stood there, gripping the frame of the bed. When Katy slowly looked up, the sadness she saw there tore at her heart. "Mom, please. Be happy for me."

Emily turned her head to the side as if she needed to steady herself, thinking as she shut her eyes. "Okay." She lifted her hand in the air and then let it fall to her side before looking over to Katy.

"Great, so no talk tomorrow?" Katy said hopefully, but her mom was shaking her head as she walked over to the door. She set her hand on the frame as she glanced back.

"Oh no, that talk will still happen, Katy. I ask you and Steven to listen to Brad, to us, and then…" Her mom said nothing else, just allowed a smile to touch her lips. "Good night, Katy," she said, and she pulled the door closed behind her.

CHAPTER
Eight

Steven was on his knees in a crawlspace, replacing a faulty switch for a heat pump. It was a simple enough job, but he'd been distracted most of the morning, which wasn't a good thing when he was trying to impress his boss and prove he was a shining star and would be an asset to his company.

"Steven!" the man shouted, and Steven banged his head when he looked up through the cutout in the floor at his round-faced boss, Hank Miller.

"Shit," he said, and he noted the frown on his boss's face.

"You almost done there? Got an emergency call on the job site outside of town."

"Yeah, almost finished." He rubbed his head and then put his tools back in his kit, slipped up through the crawlspace, and moved the floorboard back in place. "It's an odd place to stick wiring and switches.

If it floods down there it's going to be a nightmare, and someone's going to get electrocuted."

"Not up to you. We just fix it," Hank said. "Some of these old places were built sticking things in places no manner of common sense can conjure."

His boss was already out the door, and Steven noticed the piled wiring. Before his boss could ask him to grab it, Steven had it looped over his shoulder and was out the door, following Hank to the company van.

"So, Mr. Miller, I'm getting married," he said. Geez, did that sound stupid, and he wondered by the smile that touched his boss's lips, the weather-worn lines around his eyes deepening, whether he was happy for him or laughing.

"Young, you are. Congratulations. In my old age, nineteen seems so much younger than in my day. I was twenty when I got married, thought I knew everything. In fact, I knew nothing. Hope it works out for you." He pulled the side door of the van closed and went around the truck.

Steven knew he needed to get something from his boss for a commitment of work. It was now or never. He opened the door and climbed in the passenger side. "You see, Katy, that's my fiancée, and I are getting married this summer. I got us a small place in town and, well, I just wanted to ask you about after my apprenticeship. I know you said it was possible and likely I'd have full-time employment..." He stopped talking when his boss started the older van and slipped it in drive.

Hank wasn't saying a word, nothing, as he looked

at the road. His thick dark hair was in need of a cut, and his face showed dark whiskers much like it always did. Steven was positive that man needed to shave twice a day. He fisted his hands as he sat in the seat, waiting in excruciating agony. His boss then rubbed his chin and put his hand back on the steering wheel, looking out the window as if he hadn't heard a thing.

"Mr. Miller?" he added again, a show of respect he was trying to emphasize, but then how did one go about begging for a job?

"Can't give you any promises, Steven, but if business holds and you continue working as hard and showing as much promise as you have, there could be a permanent position for you." He glanced to Steven, lifting his hand from the wheel and back again, gripping it hard and then relaxing. "That's the best I can do. Sorry, but one thing I don't do is make promises for down the road when I don't know what's around the corner. One day at a time. I know it doesn't help you and the pretty young thing's security, but you're young, and you'll bounce back and figure things out. Okay?" he added as if Steven was to readily agree.

"Yeah, sure," he said, but it wasn't. There was one thing Steven had wanted to accomplish before sitting down with Brad and Emily and Katy tonight: He had wanted to be able to provide a guarantee that he would have full-time employment and the income to support a wife.

He felt a hand pat his chest. "Cheer up, kid. It's not that bad. Would you rather I lie to you and make a promise just so you feel better? Life doesn't work that way, and you better learn early on that the only person you can count on is you."

As Steven looked over at his boss, a man who seemed as if he had things together, he wondered why he'd say something like that to him. Maybe he was right that it was better to have the truth, but right now he'd rather have the man tell him what he wanted to hear.

Nine

"Brad, we should call Steven's parents, invite them over. Maybe they could sit down with Steven and Katy, too, and the four of us can persuade them to at least wait a year." Emily was pacing in the kitchen in front of Brad. Dinner was in a crockpot on the counter: a chicken stew, which, as with everything Emily made, smelled so good.

"We should sit down with them, but not tonight. Nights in the restaurant business, you know, they're working, busy in the evening. Hopefully we'll be able to get them to see reason tonight before this goes any further." Brad reached over to the cutting board, where Emily had sliced up carrots, cucumbers, and cauliflower, and grabbed a handful to munch on.

"I hope they'll listen, but I'm afraid Katy isn't going to be as accommodating. It's Steven you're going to have to reach, get him to see the wisdom in waiting."

The screen door squeaked, and Brad looked

around the corner to see Katy and Steven walk in together. She dumped her backpack at the door, and Steven was still in his work uniform, his hair a little messy and some grime on his clothes.

"Hey, how was your day?" Brad asked. He tossed a piece of carrot in his mouth and chewed.

"It was school, Dad, but I loved driving my new car. Thanks again." Katy lifted her keys and dangled them as she walked up to Brad and stopped beside him. He slid his arm around Katy, and she leaned against him. He did kiss the top of her head.

"Talk before or after dinner?" Brad said, and she rolled her eyes at him.

"Before. Let's get this over with so we can talk about the wedding."

Brad looked over to Emily, whose expression was, for the first time, resigned. Steven said nothing and just stood there at the sound of footsteps on the stairs.

"When's dinner, Mom?" Becky called out, carrying Jack.

"Half an hour," Brad said. "We're going to talk to your sister and Steven for a bit. You go upstairs and keep Jack with you, play with him."

Trevor walked in from Brad's office, and before he could ask about dinner, because it was that time of night, Brad said, "Dinner's later. Go grab a book and read in your room."

Trevor frowned, paused, and then sighed. "Fine," he said, then turned away and walked upstairs.

Steven was already sitting in the living room on

the sofa, quiet, unusually so. Katy walked over and sat right beside him, holding his hand.

"Em?" Brad said. He gestured toward her and waited as she walked into the living room and sat on the loveseat. He slid his hand over her back and shoulder, touching her, and then sat, leaning forward, his elbows resting on his knees, his hands linked together. Emily was touching him, her hand sliding around his arm, looking to him.

Steven and Katy said nothing as everyone seemed to just look at Brad, watching, waiting for him to say his peace. Where to start to get these kids to listen, to understand?

"When you're young, you believe you know everything, and everyone who's older tries to tell you how to think, feel, act," Brad said. "They say they know better and you should listen. As I can see now, Katy, you're already starting to shut down and no longer listen to a word I say. Just stop and take a breath. Steven," he said, gesturing to the young man who was watching him and maybe wondering what he was going to say next. "Well, I'm not going to tell either of you what you should do, because I did the same thing as a young and arrogant man, thinking I knew better, but I didn't. I suffered the consequences, learning the hard way, and maybe that's what you two need to do."

"Dad," Katy started, and Brad noticed Steven squeeze her hand to stop her.

"Katy, let's just hear what your dad has to say," he said. Steven surprised Brad, and that was something not many people did.

Katy nodded and turned those light blue eyes to Brad and then over to Emily, her hand holding Steven's as she sat pressed against him.

"My father tried to warn me," Brad said, "to give me advice about marrying my first wife, but I wouldn't listen. Everything my father said was right, but I was too proud to listen, and then for years I allowed the rift between us to grow. I don't want that here." He gestured between them and looked down to Emily, who he could tell was thinking a lot of things, none of which were making her happy.

"Katy, we love you and just want the best for you," Emily added. "You don't know how your dad has looked after us, after you, Becky, Trevor, and Jack, so none of us have ever had to worry about anything. It's just that I worry you have no life experience, no way to deal with whatever problems life decides to toss your way, because we've sheltered you."

Katy was tensing up again, and even Steven seemed to feel that was too much. Brad recognized the look, as if they knew better, so he glanced back to Emily. She knew, of course, as she squeezed his arm.

"We've said our peace," Brad said. "I guess what we need to hear from you is what your plan is. You say you have a place you've rented in town. You're not both looking to move in here or with your parents, Steven. How about jobs, your future?" Brad added, waiting for them to start talking. Katy, for the first time, seemed at a loss for words as she looked to Steven.

"I'm picking up the keys to my new place after we

finish here," Steven said. "It's small. After I finish my apprenticeship, I'll be making good money, and we'd like to have a place like this one day—smaller, nothing this big, but something that's ours."

Steven was idealistic. What could Brad say to them, both of them? "Katy, what about you and school? You've goofed off and blown this last semester, and now you have to retake almost everything."

"I told you I'll retake those courses. I can do it at night in the fall and work during the day," she said.

"You know there's an easier solution. You go back to school in the fall, retake those courses, and then in six months you can get married," Brad said, but he already knew she wouldn't consider it. Steven said nothing as he sat beside her and then turned his head to her. She just shook her head. She could be so darn stubborn. At least he had tried. "Well, then, I guess the next step is to talk about your wedding."

Katy couldn't get over how her dad and mom had come around, and she hadn't expected for them to be this supportive. When she'd brought up moving in with Steven now, though, before the wedding, Brad had said absolutely not. Not that her mom would have considered the matter, but they made it clear she was getting married in August and she would live at the ranch until then. It was extremely old fashioned, but Brad had said that for a girl as young as Katy, getting married at eighteen was one thing, but moving in with Steven now was another altogether.

Instead of pushing the matter, she and Steven had both let it slide.

Katy opened a box and unwrapped the glasses inside, old hand-me-downs from Steven's parents. As she took in the small galley kitchen in the tiny apartment Steven had rented, with its mustard-yellow carpeting in the living room and chipped tile in the kitchen, she couldn't shake a sense of excitement. This was going to be her place, just hers and Steven's, and the weeks were ticking down. It was a new life, a new start, and being married to Steven was going to be perfect.

"This is the last box, all my old dishes. Glad at least they can be put to use," Steven's mom said. Lydia was slim and curvy, with a generous bust and a curvy butt that was astonishingly bigger than anything Katy had seen. She rarely smiled, and Katy wondered whether she really liked her.

"Thank you. We'll use them proudly," she said. She wanted to give her head a shake, but making small talk wasn't easy with someone you weren't comfortable with. Where was Steven? He should have been there by now. What was taking him and his dad so long?

"Maybe I should go and give Steven and his dad a hand bringing that sofa up," Katy said just as she heard them on the stairs outside the door.

Lydia was already there and then outside in the hallway. "Dez, careful you don't catch the sides," she said. She was directing them, taking charge, and Katy was getting the feeling Steven's mom didn't think she belonged there.

She stood back, watching as Steven and his dad lugged in an older sofa with stiff black and gold cushions and set it down in the empty living room. Steven didn't have a TV, but he had a bed that took up just about the entire small bedroom. The six-drawer dresser took up the rest, leaving not much room to walk around.

"How about this, son? Your very first place," Dez said. Steven's dad wasn't particularly handsome at first sight, but there was something about the man. As Katy had gotten to know him and his quiet ways, she had realized he was driven in his career, running his restaurant, and confident in everything he did. His dark hair was graying, and his large nose and cheeks were pockmarked from a bad case of acne during his teenage years, but his eyes startled Katy. They weren't just brown but so dark they were almost black, showing his mixed heritage. He was tall and solid, a few inches shorter than Brad.

Katy hung back and opened up the taped box of dishes.

"Oh, be careful with those, Katy," Lydia said. "They may be old, but they've been in my family for a lot of years. Every piece is intact."

Steven looked over to her. Katy felt inadequate around his mom, and Dez said nothing as he watched her and then Steven.

"Katy, come on over here and try out the sofa," Steven called out. Maybe that was his way of lightening the mood.

"Well, we should be going," Lydia said. "We still have to get things prepped before the restaurant opens for dinner." She reached out and kissed Steven's cheek, and his dad smiled and rested his hand on Steven's shoulder. Then both his parents left, and Dez waved and took Katy in as he followed his wife out the door. She wasn't sure if he was saying goodbye to her or just generally, so she did what she'd been taught. "Goodbye, Mr. and Mrs. Bennett," she said, and she stopped herself from saying *Thanks for helping Steven.* That last part she knew wouldn't be welcomed at all.

As the door closed, Steven slid his arms around her waist and pulled her closer.

"Your parents don't like me," she said, feeling his hands loosen from where they'd settled on the curve of her butt. Then he pushed away and ran his hands over his head. His hair was sticking up at the back. There were days she could tell he'd just gotten up and dressed without combing his hair, and this was one of them.

"Katy, you're being ridiculous and reading into things," he said. "She just doesn't know you, and it's not as if you haven't reached out. You close up when Mom's around. She just doesn't know how to talk to you. Maybe you should call her up and go for lunch or something, maybe talk to her about some of the wedding plans."

Steven was at the door and pulling it open. He had to go to work even though it was his sixth day on and she wished he had the day off. He now had his own place, their place, and they were alone. She walked over to him and stepped closer, rising up on her tiptoes as she slid her arms around his neck. She could feel every hard inch of him, which she'd felt and touched for what felt like forever. She had seen every part of him but had never felt him inside her. It would be perfect now.

"You could call in sick, and we could test out your bed," she said. She touched her lips to his, and of course he responded. He always did, wrapping her tongue around his, her fingers in his hair around the back of his head.

He pulled her closer, and her legs went around him as he lifted her. Her breasts pressed to his chest, aching to be touched. Then he broke the kiss, still holding her. He groaned and said, "I can't, Katy. I call in sick, I lose my chance of a permanent job. I need this. We need this."

"But we've never been alone, and now we have this."

"We will," Steven said. He slid his hand under her thigh so she'd loosen her legs, and she slid down his front, feeling every hard part of him again. "I just…" He looked up as if he needed to think of a reason. "You and I both know that your dad would kill me. I can't believe I'm going to say this, but maybe we should wait. We're getting married soon, and our first night together…do you really want something rushed in the bedroom with me out the door five minutes later?"

Why did he have to put it like that? Right now she didn't want to consider that option. She just wanted to feel close with Steven, to make love with him, to finally feel and understand what it was to be a woman. They'd come so close a few times, but her family was always somewhere in the background, even the times they had snuck off to the hayloft.

"I'm not agreeing, but I'll let you get back to work," Katy said. "Maybe I'll stay here and finish unpacking the dishes, organizing things." She wanted to put her mark on the place, arrange everything her way.

Steven hesitated. "Mom is actually coming back here later this afternoon to bring a few more things, and you have school, remember?" He ushered her out the door and locked it, pocketing the keys.

She stared at the door and then Steven. "You didn't give me a key."

He stopped. "Um, yeah, I have to get another cut. I'll do that later. Besides, you're not moving in yet. After we're married." He reached for her hand, and she followed him down the stairs to her yellow Beetle. As she climbed in and started the car, she watched him slide behind the wheel of his Cavalier and pull away.

Katy couldn't shake the fact that the door was locked, yet his mother was coming back to set up their home—so his mother had a key and Katy didn't. Steven was letting his mom step in and arrange his life, set up his home, without a thought to Katy's wants. Yeah, this could definitely be a problem.

"So you're letting them get married," Neil said.

Brad hadn't heard him drive in as he walked out of the barn, carrying two bales of hay, and loaded it in the back of the trailer attached to the tractor. "Can't see how we can stop them, Neil." He pulled off his leather gloves and tucked them in his back pocket, taking in the midday sun and looking over to the house, where he knew Emily was inside with Jack, caring for him and pulling out ideas for the wedding so she could go over them with Katy later on.

"You could tell her no. She's just a kid, and I can't believe I'm going to say this, but let her move in with him and wait to get married." Neil rested his arm over the wooden rail of the trailer. His dark hair had a few more threads of gray and was now touching the edges of his ears. He was, though, still dressed in faded jeans and a light T-shirt.

"Telling her no is only going to have her digging

her heels in more and maybe doing something really stupid." Brad tossed Neil his gloves, which he caught one handed. "Give me a hand. Need to fill this trailer and get over to Cliff, to the other barn in the south field."

"You keeping the cows out there now?" Neil asked, not that he kept up with what was going on in Brad's world on the ranch. Neil was about business, not ranching. Even though he knew his way around the livestock and could, if need be, step in and help out, it just wasn't in his blood like it was in Brad's.

"For the summer. Not much grazing up here. Better closer to the hills." Brad grabbed another pair of work gloves from the bin inside the barn and lifted another two bales, then walked around Neil. Brad heard him grunt as he lifted two bales of hay himself, as well. "A little out of shape there, Neil?" He couldn't resist.

"Can keep up with you, old man!" Neil said, tossing the bales on the trailer and then hopping up to stack them. Then he was staring at the house, deep in thought.

"Candy here?" Brad asked.

Neil gestured with an incline of his head. "She's helping Emily, talking about plans for the wedding and something about Katy's gown for graduation."

It had been all Katy had talked of for the past month, the graduation gown she had to have. She and Emily had gone on a shopping trip, and he'd never seen the dress but knew they'd bought it.

"I don't know how this isn't driving you nuts,"

Neil said. "I'd have locked Katy in her room and forbidden her to leave." He flashed a big grin.

"No, you wouldn't have, because when it's your turn you'll realize you can't run her life or tell her what to do. She's determined, and Steven…it's not like he just started hanging around. He's been in the picture since she was fifteen. I just never expected it to happen like this."

"So you're letting them get married, and when it falls apart, when the going gets rough and they figure out they're too young and she comes running home, then what?" Neil asked.

Brad had wondered the same thing. It would happen, and he and Em couldn't step in and solve their problems. At the same time, he didn't want her to think he wouldn't be there for her. "Not a choice, Neil. Keep thinking about me and Dad, remember?"

Of course everyone did. Neil winced.

"At least Steven isn't anything like Crystal," Brad said. "He's got a lot going for him, and maybe they'll surprise us." He couldn't even make himself believe it, though.

"Seriously? This is a different generation, Brad. Times are different, and getting married at eighteen is just unheard of now."

He heard a car and turned his head to the driveway, seeing a silver newer Buick pull in.

"You expecting someone?" Neil asked.

In the distance, Brad could see a man with light hair, a round face, and glasses step out of the vehicle.

He didn't need to be closer to know who it was: Emily's ex, Katy's father.

"Isn't that…?" Neil started.

"Yeah, Bob Nelson, Emily's ex. Better go see what he wants," Brad said as he started to the house, hearing, from where he walked, the knock on the front door.

Steven's phone was ringing, but by the time he put down his tools and pulled it from his back pocket, it had stopped. That was when he noticed the number of missed calls and three voice-mails. The first one was from Katy, something about his mom. He wasn't sure what she was going on about. Then there was a message from his mom that just said, "Call me." The last was from Katy again, and as he listened, he picked up something about her dad having shown up. She too ended with "Call me."

"You finish with those sockets yet?" Hank strode into the sunroom he'd contracted from a couple who were adding on to their home. Steven was just finishing wiring the three sockets when his boss went over and started checking his work.

"This is the last one," he said.

Hank grunted and then adjusted something, and Steven looked over, worried for a minute that he'd messed something up. "Looks good," Hank said. "You may as well pack up your stuff and head on home. That's the last of it for today." He paused. "Listen, I wanted to talk to you. Things are slowing down a bit for me, and I just wanted to give you a heads up that when you finish your apprenticeship, unless business picks up, I may not be able to keep you on."

This wasn't what he wanted to hear. He was getting married, he'd just rented a place, and he couldn't be suddenly unemployed. "But it's not for sure?" Steven said hopefully.

His boss didn't smile. He wasn't a man who made a lot of big gestures. He did, though, take his time and think things through. "Not for certain. Don't know what the future holds, Steven. That's one thing to keep in mind about life, son: Nothing is a sure thing. Just thought you should know, just in case you need to make plans." Hank then patted his shoulder before striding out, and Steven couldn't keep the worry from biting up his back. Plans…what plans could he make? He could keep his options open, put feelers out for another job.

His phone was ringing again. He didn't look to see who was calling before he answered. "Hello?" he said, sighing, pressing his hand to his forehead just as he heard Katy's voice.

"Where are you? Why haven't you called me back? I've been waiting here for you to call. This is an absolute disaster—"

"Katy, I'm working. I can't just take a call whenever you phone. I kind of want to keep my job. What is going on?" He couldn't remember her ever sounding this upset.

"My dad showed up—you know, my real dad, not Brad."

How could he forget Bob Nelson? Aside from being Katy's father, though, the man wouldn't have left a lasting impression. He was a simple man who blended into the background, one Steven knew cared for Katy, but he wasn't Brad, who made sure his family was his first and last thought and did everything he did each day for his kids, his wife. Brad was the kind of man he wanted to be, the kind of man Katy's real dad was not.

"Well, what does he want?" Steven said as he walked out of the sunroom and waved to his boss, who was loading up the van. Steven opened his car door as he unfastened his tool belt.

"He's angry because he just found out from the school that I failed my courses." She sighed on the other end.

Steven couldn't believe Katy had slacked off, either. She'd told him before her finals, when she should have been studying, that she had no intention of putting anything extra into it, as they were getting married and she wasn't pursuing anything postsecondary. That was fine with him, but he hadn't realized she meant she wouldn't be putting any effort into her final reports. "Well, you're making the classes up in the fall at night. Your mom and dad know, so what's the problem?" He dumped his tool belt in the back-seat and slid behind the wheel.

"The problem is that he showed up here and upset Mom. I got home, and Dad was in Mom's face about how she doesn't share anything with him. Mrs. Moore apparently reached out to him and told him I was getting married." She sighed on the other end. "I've never seen him so upset."

He knew she hadn't told her dad yet. She had planned to in person the following week when she saw him at her graduation.

"Listen, I'm just finishing up. I'll swing by," he said.

"That would be great. Oh, and I wanted to talk to you about something else. I stopped by your place on the way home from school and ran into your mom."

He wanted to pull the phone away and stare into it. "Katy, I told you Mom was going by this afternoon, and I have a message from Mom to call her. Did something happen?"

"I just tried to arrange the place the way I wanted it. It's our home, Steven, but your mom seems to have different ideas," Katy said. The last thing he wanted was to be a referee between his mom and Katy.

"Okay, great…" What else could he say? He started his car. "I'll be there soon."

He hung up, wondering why Katy was pushing so hard with his mom. He knew his mom was still upset that he was getting married, and she had put Katy down, too, wondering whether she was pregnant.

They just needed to give his mom some space. As he'd learned growing up, she'd eventually come around on just about everything. The only problem was that sometimes it took far longer than he and his dad were comfortable with.

Thirteen

Bob Nelson was a selfish prick, in Brad's book. He'd never liked the man, and he knew and understood how Emily hated having any contact with him at all. He'd never once treated Emily with an ounce of respect since she'd been with Brad. He undermined her, always behind her back in subtle and cowardly ways that Brad still had trouble wrapping his head around.

Now Bob was standing in Brad's living room, accusing Emily of not doing enough for Katy and of hiding from him the fact that his very young daughter, who'd only just turned eighteen, was planning on getting married.

"Bob, I told you before that I haven't kept anything from you. It's Katy's responsibility to tell you, and she was planning on sharing her news next week." Emily was standing with her arms crossed stiffly, and Brad could see the tension across her shoulders.

"You should have told me! She's too young. I had to find out from her teacher."

Right now Brad was of a mind to call this teacher up and maybe the principal, too, about all the moral lines they'd just crossed. Did they have no idea how impressionable young kids viewed their behavior? Honest was honest, and this was backstabbing. Katy getting married wasn't that teacher's business to share.

"Dad, this isn't Mom's fault," Katy said. "Don't blame her." She was kneeling on the loveseat, her arms draped over the back. Candy was beside her and kept exchanging glances with Neil, who was leaning in the archway to the kitchen, watching Michael as he raced a car around on the carpet.

"Katy, you are too young to get married," Bob said. "I'm not quite sure where you'd get the idea this is okay. And school! You need an education. Didn't your mom help you with your homework and follow up with the school to make sure you were keeping up your grades?"

Brad was watching Jack as he crawled across the floor to the coffee table, pulling himself up and walking around it. He tried to figure what it was Bob was trying to accomplish. Upsetting Emily? Yes, he believed the man was so angry with her still for divorcing him and ending his comfortable life that it didn't matter what she did; it would never be good enough.

"Katy is a big girl and is responsible for her own grades, for her own decisions," Brad said from where he leaned against the sofa table, his arms crossed.

"She failed, and she has to make up the courses. It's not up to anybody to make Katy do something she doesn't want to. She has to motivate herself. She's getting married, and you can't make her decisions for her."

He could hear a car, and Katy jumped up.

"Steven's here," she said, and she ran to the door. The silence that filled the room ratcheted up the tension a few notches.

"Bob, why don't you sit down?" Brad said, because standing here was only adding to the stress. The man was far from reasonable.

Emily gave him a look, and it was only times like this when he saw her insecurity. Then again, Bob never said anything good about Emily, only talked about how the things she did always inconvenienced him in some way. Bob did step over to the sofa, but he didn't sit as the screen door squeaked and both Katy and Steven walked in.

"Steven, how are you? How was work today?" Brad added, maybe to somehow bring reasonableness back into the conversation.

Steven just took everyone in for a second. His eyes widened as he looked to Brad and then over to Neil, who lifted his hand to wave but didn't say a word. "It was good," he said, holding Katy's hand. "Mr. Nelson, good to see you again." He reached out to Bob, who seemed to hesitate a second before accepting the handshake.

Good job, Brad wanted to say to Steven, but he held his tongue.

"I'm not understanding how you two seem to think you can just get married. Katy doesn't even have her high school diploma yet. Are you living here? What do you plan to do with my daughter, and who's paying for this?" he added, frowning, shoving his hands in his front pockets.

Katy said nothing, and Brad hated seeing the hurt on her face.

"I am," Brad said before Emily could say a word. "She's my daughter. Of course I'm paying for her wedding."

He saw relief on Katy's face. She couldn't hide anything.

"We haven't even talked about plans for the wedding yet," Emily said, "but don't worry, Bob, there will be no cost to you. You're off the hook."

Her ex should have been happy, but he looked even more miserable. "You know I would love to pay for her wedding. I'm her father, but I haven't had an easy life like you, Emily."

Brad heard Neil swear behind him, and he turned to see his brother shaking his head.

"Let me be clear," Bob said. "You can pay for this, but I'm her father. I'm giving her away."

No one in the room said a word. Brad wanted to argue and say otherwise, but as he waited for Katy to say something different, he realized this might be something he had no say in at all.

CHAPTER
Fourteen

"You're not staying for dinner?" Katy said to Steven as they watched her father drive away. She was uneasy still from his visit, and she didn't know how to ease the stress he'd brought into the house.

Steven slid his arm around Katy's waist and leaned down to kiss her. He seemed distant, and she wasn't sure why. Maybe he too was upset with her, and she felt as if she was making a mess out of everything.

"No, I've got to go finish setting up my place and meet Mom and Dad at their restaurant for dinner. Just got a text." He held up his phone.

It wasn't lost on Katy that he hadn't asked her to go with him, and she wondered if the hurt showed on her face. "I see," she said. She stepped away, and maybe he'd noticed or figured it out, because he suddenly appeared mad, and that wasn't something Steven ever did with her.

"Look, Katy, I'm not sure what happened today with you and Mom, and I'm not sure why you went back there when I told you Mom was stopping back in."

Katy took another step back and just looked up at Steven. How could she explain that she was embarrassed about how she'd behaved, but his mom had become so territorial when she'd walked into his place, knowing she was there? She had even almost rubbed in the fact that she had a key and Katy didn't, which was odd.

"Okay, Steven, maybe you don't get this, but it isn't okay to have another woman come in, even if it's your mother, and arrange your place, which is going to be ours. You have your mom putting her touches on something that should be mine. We're getting married. This is our life. I don't understand how you can allow your mother to just step in as if she's part of this."

Katy was flustered, and she could hear talking inside. She knew she'd screwed up with her family, too. This wasn't her day, and she didn't know how to say something to Brad, to her mom. She'd been in shock and hadn't been able to get her tongue to move when her dad had announced he was giving her away. It was something she'd thought of, but she'd never considered for one moment that Brad wouldn't be there to walk her down the aisle. She didn't know how to tell Bob how she felt, though. She didn't want to hurt him.

Steven rested his hand on Katy's shoulder and

then stepped in, lowered his head, and brushed his lips to hers. "Okay, I get it. I'll talk to my mom, but please go easy," he said, then kissed her again before glancing at the door. "You know that wasn't cool what your dad did, expecting Brad to pay and then saying he's giving you away. Did you see Brad's face, your mom's? Katy, you need to say something, to speak up. But that's your call, your family, your dad."

"I froze, Steven. I didn't know what to say. I feel bad for my dad finding out the way he did, and of course he's hurt. I just didn't expect him to show up here. I just want everyone to get along, and…"

She wished Brad would just tell her he'd handle it, but that wouldn't be fair. He was the reasonable one, the father she leaned on, depended on, the one who would always be there for her. He was the one she'd always call and go to if she were in trouble. It wasn't even a question.

"This has to be your decision, Katy. I feel bad for Brad, and I didn't expect him to pay for our wedding. I'm talking to Mom and Dad about that, too. Maybe they'll pitch in for the reception dinner, the food. You need to go and smooth things over, though. I hate to tell you this, but considering the way your dad showed up here, throwing his weight around, I was embarrassed for him. To me it seemed it was more about the money."

Of course it was. It always had been. Katy knew that deep down, considering her dad had never provided anything for her or bought her much of anything. No, it had been Brad and her mom who had given her everything. Why couldn't her dad just chill?

"I'll talk to my dad, but what about us, Steven, our wedding? We need to sit down and talk about it, plan it. Mom and Candy are inside, and they have ideas." The fact was that she was enjoying the attention and dreaming of the white dress and the fairytale wedding, for everything to be perfect.

The door squeaked open. "Hey, you two, just putting dinner out," Emily said. She still appeared tense. Her dad had always had that effect on her.

"Can't stay tonight, Mrs. Friessen. I'm sorry, I've got to meet my parents, but maybe it would be a good idea if you and Mr. Friessen and Katy and I sit down with my mom and dad."

Emily's eyes seemed to brighten, and she nodded. "Absolutely. Why don't I call your mom, Steven, and set something up? Katy?" she said before going back in the house.

As Katy watched Steven jog down to his car, she lifted her hand and waved. He pulled down the driveway and drove away, and she shut her eyes for a minute, wondering where all this conflict had come from today.

"So you're footing the bill for the wedding, and that jerk just shows up here and demands his rights?" Neil said. He was holding Jack after having gone to the school to pick up Becky and Cat. Trevor had been dropped off by one of his coworkers, as he'd been doing work experience in town, bagging groceries at the supermarket. Candy was in the kitchen with Emily, setting the kitchen table and most likely trying to lighten her mood.

"He messed with her," Brad said as he watched Emily and some of the spark that had gone out of her from Bob's little visit. Bob had somehow planted a seed of doubt in Emily, making her question whether she was responsible for this mess—which wasn't really a mess. He'd talk to her later, try to smooth things out, even though it hurt him to have to stand there and listen to the man demand to give Katy away when Brad believed she was as much his child as his other three were.

"Who?" Neil said, standing up. He lifted Jack and pressed a kiss to his tummy, and Jack giggled.

"Emily. He's always messed with her. Never talks to her, but he has this anger he's held on to for all these years. He's so unhappy, you can see it, and he especially doesn't want Emily to be happy. I could see it today."

The screen door slapped shut, and Katy appeared there. She looked uncomfortable. "I'm sorry my dad did that. I feel bad. I should have said something, but I was scared to speak up."

"Katy, your dad coming in here like that threw us all," Brad said. "I can understand him being upset, though, hearing about you getting married from your teacher."

She stepped in closer, wrapping her arms around her front. "I know, and I planned to tell him next week in person so I could show him my ring. I didn't think he'd want to give me away."

"That's your choice, Katy," Brad said.

"So you don't want to give me away?"

Brad couldn't believe she'd think that. "Are you kidding? Do you have any idea what it means for a father to give away his daughter? Of course I do. You're my child."

She seemed to relax a bit, and Brad looked to Neil, who was still shaking his head.

"You're scared to tell Bob," Neil said. "Just say the word, Katy, and I'll tell him, talk to him with you."

Brad just held up his hand to get Neil to stop.

"I don't know how to tell my dad. I know he'll be hurt, and I don't like seeing him upset," Katy said.

"But you have no trouble talking to your dad and I," Emily said as she strode out of the kitchen.

"Well, of course not. Why would I have trouble talking to you? You're my parents," Katy said as if they should know better.

Brad wanted to laugh, because she didn't get how her mom was likely to wrap her hands around her neck and shake her.

"Really, Katy?" Emily snapped.

"I'll talk to my dad. I'll tell him next week," she said and sighed, and Brad took in her uncertainty and the spooked, worried look he'd never seen in her expression before.

Steven walked right into the kitchen of the Seaside Restaurant, owned by his parents, and took in the chef, the kitchen staff, and his mom giving orders. His dad was at a table in the dining room, talking with the patrons. The restaurant was one of the better ones around, and his parents had strived for excellence, having achieved the TripAdvisor award two years running. It was, as always, a busy night.

"Mom," Steven called out, catching her attention as she was plating a dish. She said something to one of the staff, a young man he didn't recognize, and he took over.

"Steven, good timing. Your dad saved a table for us just outside the lounge, a nice ocean view." Lydia wasn't smiling, and she gestured to the chef and then said something.

Steven knew the table she had reserved. It was the best in the house, private and away from most of the others, with large picture windows overlooking the ocean and the rocky shoreline. He took a seat in the middle of the round table, knowing his parents would join him soon.

"Steven, good to see you," said Tom, the head waiter. He was young, with strawberry blond hair, neat and tall and lanky, dressed in the dining room attire of black dress pants, a white shirt, and a red tie. He set a menu in front of Steven. "Would you like a drink while waiting for your parents?"

"Whatever beer you have on tap would be great," he said knowing his parents allowed it if he was discreet, thinking he would need something before his mom joined him and started in on whatever it was Katy had done. He still wasn't sure why she couldn't get along with his girl or why Katy was pushing so hard with her.

"Did Tom get you a drink?" Dez asked as he pulled out a chair and sat down across from him. Just then, a glass filled with beer, foam on top, appeared in front of him.

"Yup," Steven said. He lifted the glass and took a swallow, listening as his mom asked for a bottle of merlot, one of the fancier labels.

He took in his parents, who were looking at each other as if they'd already spoken about something and just needed to share it with him. He should have been worried by the exchange, but right now, after his day, he just wanted to drink his beer, go home to his new place, and not worry about one more problem being dumped on him. His mom and dad said nothing as they waited and their wine was poured. Dez tasted, and then their glasses were filled.

"To mine and Katy's wedding," Steven said. He held up his glass and took in his mom's face and the fact that she wasn't raising her glass. His dad, though, seemed to think differently. He lifted his glass, touched Steven's, and then drank.

"I wanted to talk to you about Katy," Lydia said. She rested her arm on the table. Her hair was pulled back, tied at the nape, her face caked with the usual makeup she applied every night in the restaurant.

Steven said nothing as he stared at his mom. His dad, whom he glanced to, seemed to be taking this all in. He had to know what this was about, as there was little his parents didn't share with each other.

"She's rude and disrespectful," his mom said. "Walking into your place the way she did while I was organizing your kitchen…she doesn't live there yet. You know we've sat by the sidelines for the last few years while you've dated Katy, and your dad and I feel it's time we sat you down for a talk about the future and what it holds."

Steven's hand was around his glass, feeling the chilled droplets dripping down the sides. He lifted it for another taste and then glanced to his dad, who appeared lost in deep thought. He wasn't a man known for a lot of words. He was a thinker, a deep thinker. His mom was the one who did all the talking.

"Son, we're asking you to reconsider marrying this girl right now," Dez finally said. He rested his fingers on the stem of his wineglass, running up and down.

"Just for now, putting it off a few years. Maybe date some other girls…"

"Dad, I love Katy, and we're getting married August 18. Brad and Emily have even come around. You don't have to like Katy. It would be nice if you did, but I'm marrying her, so don't start this now about how you don't like her or want me to date other girls as if I don't know what I want." He went to move his chair back, put some distance between him and everything about this day, which was going from bad to worse.

His dad reached out and grabbed his wrist. "Stop. Don't walk away mad. I'm just asking for you to hear us out. You've never dated another girl or been steady with one as long as Katy. We just thought it was an infatuation that would blow over, but I see how wrong we were."

Steven rested his palm on the table and took in his mom, who had fisted her hand and lifted it to rest her chin on.

"Steven, just listen—"

"I'm so sorry to be late," said someone behind him. Steven looked up to see a young woman, tall and slender, with a generous bust and dark hair that hung in soft waves past her shoulders. She was wearing a dark blue dress that was simple, tasteful, with cap sleeves. She had a square jaw and bold blue eyes and a smile that lit up the room.

"Oh, Casey, so glad you could make it," Lydia said. Dez pulled out a chair, and the young lady sat. "Steven, I want you to meet Casey Richards. Her

family moved here just last year. She's studying jour-
nalism. Her father and your dad are old friends who
lost touch and just reconnected."

Steven inclined his head, taking in Casey,
wondering why this seemed so odd. He was here to
discuss his wedding.

"Your parents told me so much about you, Steven.
Said you went to trade school to be an electrician.
What made you want to do that?" She was polite,
pretty, and she smiled up at Tom as he set an empty
wine glass in front of her. Dez filled her glass. "Thank
you," she said.

"I like the hands-on aspect. Trade school I think is
a good choice when you're not looking for a business
degree, which I wasn't. I love working with my
hands."

"Would you two excuse us?" his mother said and
gestured to his dad as they both slid back their chairs.
"We just need to take care of a few things. You two
talk."

He was about to say he was tired, but he did have
good manners, and that would be rude in front of
Casey. Why was she here? Then it dawned on him:
the timing. It was so obvious.

Steven lifted his beer and swallowed half of it
down. "Just curious why my parents invited you for
dinner," he said. He knew it sounded rude, but he
really hoped this wasn't a setup, their idea of putting a
pretty girl in front of him and hoping he'd consider
straying to take her out. It was low.

She opened her mouth to say something and

seemed to be struggling to think of what to say. "Um, this is awkward. They thought I might like to meet you, two singles the same age."

Steven was shaking his head. "The thing is, Casey, I'm not single. In fact, I'm getting married in August to a pretty girl who stole my heart. It seems my parents have other ideas." He actually lifted his glass of beer and swallowed the rest. "You seem like a nice girl, Casey," he said as he slid back his chair. Then he stood up, taking in the alarm on the young woman's face, and started toward the door.

What was up with Steven? He'd never called her after dinner with his parents, and she'd expected him to call this morning like he did every morning, but he hadn't.

"What's up, Katy?" Brad stepped out onto the front porch. It was Saturday, late morning, and Emily had left with Becky and Jack, taking Brad's truck over to Candy and Neil's. She'd asked Katy if she'd like to come too, but Katy had been too busy sulking and considering all manner of scenarios to explain why Steven hadn't called.

It was obsessive, she knew that, but this wasn't something Steven normally did.

"Hi, Dad, just sitting." She shrugged from where she sat in the comfortable wicker chair, her feet tucked under her to the side, as she was still in her pajama bottoms and top.

Her dad frowned and took in the yard and porch as he strode to the rail, then took his time turning around and leaning back. His faded jeans were smudged with dirt, and his light blue shirt had a few spots—of what, she wasn't sure. His sleeves were rolled up, and she could see how strong his forearms were, so different from Steven's.

"You've been quiet all morning. Noticed you've checked your phone a dozen times or so." He gestured toward it.

"Haven't heard from Steven since his dinner with his parents last night. He always calls every morning," she said. Brad was actually trying not to laugh, and it didn't make her happy. "Dad, this isn't funny. Something has to be wrong. I called him and he still hasn't called me back."

"Katy, he's probably busy. He's got a job, full time, and just moved into his own place. Don't start reading something into it. I'm sure he'll tell you the same thing."

No, he was wrong. She and Steven talked every day, but last night had been odd. "Steven had dinner with his parents last night, and I wasn't invited," she said, watching the way her dad seemed to take her in. She didn't have a clue what he was thinking.

He looked to the side, maybe considering what he needed to say. "It happens, Katy. It's not a big deal. Maybe they just wanted some time alone with their son. You know we too like having just us here for dinner, just family."

"But Steven has always been welcome here. Mom always sets a place for him. She's never not invited him. Lydia doesn't like me," she said, sighing deeply.

Her dad was watching her again, and he wasn't smiling. "What's going on?" he asked.

She shrugged. What could she say? The woman had never been the type to pull her aside and sit one on one for girl time to get to know her. "I stopped by Steven's yesterday before coming home, and his mom was there. She was organizing his kitchen, and I wanted to do it myself. It will be my kitchen, mine and Steven's. She made me feel as if I didn't belong. But even before that, she's never really been friendly. Not like you and Mom are with Steven."

"Katy, Steven's mom is just that, his mom. Sounds like you may have overstepped a bit yesterday."

She couldn't believe her dad had said that, and maybe her face said how well she was taking his comment.

He leaned forward, touched her arm, and shook it gently. "Hey, just listen a second. You are a great kid, kind, thoughtful, respectful, but as far as Steven is concerned, you have been all about him for years. Sometimes with women you need to tread carefully. Some are territorial about their kids, family, everything."

She wasn't sure she understood what Brad was saying, but didn't he get the fact that Steven's mother could be a problem? "How do I get Steven to see his mom as the problem she is? I think she would be happy if I would go away, and she's never once congratulated us on our upcoming wedding."

"Katy, you can't ever try to break the bond or come between Steven and his family. His mom is his, and you need to just let her get to know you. Don't push so hard, and who cares about the kitchen? The day it becomes yours, just move everything where you want it."

Katy heard a car and looked over to see Steven driving in. She put her hands to her hair, which she had simply pinned up. She still needed to get cleaned up, so before Steven could get out of the car, she jumped up and raced into the house and up the stairs to grab a shower and get dressed.

Eighteen

Brad shouldn't have laughed, but Katy's face when Steven had driven in had been priceless. He could hear the shower running upstairs now as Steven, dressed in faded jeans and a T-shirt of some local band, stared at the door with a puzzled expression.

"She didn't expect you to just drive in. She's getting dressed," Brad said.

"Do you have a second to talk, Mr. Friessen?" Steven asked. When Brad gestured for him to come in, he said, "No, do you mind if we stay out here?"

Brad wasn't sure, but it looked as if something was bothering Steven. "Everything okay?" he asked. "Heard you had dinner with your parents last night."

Steven seemed to need a minute to gather himself. "Okay, but it seems they had other ideas," Steven said. He seemed genuinely distressed.

"Oh," Brad replied. He wasn't sure what was up, but he also knew Emily was still planning on having the parents over to sit down and get to know each other better, talk about the wedding.

"Mom and Katy don't really get along. I just ignored it, but you know Katy. Sometimes she pushes," he said. "And Mom, she's always been a little difficult. I just hadn't realized she'd taken such a disliking to Katy."

Brad had never considered for a moment that Katy might have been right, since one of the things she did often was blow everything way out of proportion. Maybe she hadn't been so off after all. "This doesn't sound good. I didn't know."

"I never did either. Just thought it was Katy reading too much into things, but last night at dinner, which didn't happen, by the way, my parents seemed to be keen on me dating other women, postponing the wedding. They even went so far as to set me up and have another girl my age join us for dinner. I never expected them to do something like that."

Considering all the things Brad had considered doing to try to convince Katy to take some time and wait instead of jumping into marriage, he too would have loved to see her date some other boys, but he'd never once thought of setting her up with one. He wasn't sure how to feel about that.

"You're not saying much. I'm pretty angry with my parents," Steven said, shoving his hands in his pockets. Brad recognized the emotion, the anger, the hurt that seemed to be a part of Steven. It was that sort of young hotheaded emotion that could end up dividing a family.

"Not saying it was okay for your parents to do that, but just take some advice, Steven. Don't do anything rash. You may need to talk to your parents again, sit them down. They had their reasons, but I'm not even going to try to figure them out for the life of me. You and your parents need to keep some peace, but at the same time they have to respect your choice. They don't have to like it, but take some time and think about it calmly before sitting down with them."

Steven's phone must have been on vibrate, as he pulled it out, looked at it, and then pressed a button before slipping it back in his pocket. "My mom. She's been calling since I walked out on that date at the restaurant last night."

"You were on a date?" Katy said.

Brad hadn't heard her come out, but she was standing there just inside the screen door, looking out. She pushed open the door, her wet hair brushed back and hanging straight, wearing a jean skirt and a blue tank top. There was such emotion in her eyes that he expected her to burst into tears.

"No, it wasn't like that, Katy. I got to the restaurant last night for dinner, and my mom and dad surprised me." Steven was talking fast and trying to get through to Katy as she reached for the ring on her finger. Brad could see the moment she was pulling it off.

"Katy, you need to listen to Steven," Brad said, but although he wanted to stay there and handle this, the two kids needed to figure it out together, because if they couldn't communicate now, where would they be in a few months down the road after they were married?

Brad rested his hands on Katy's shoulders, slid his finger under her chin, and lifted just until she looked up at him with tears pooled in her young, innocent eyes. "Oh, Katy, wish I could protect you from all this, but you need to talk, and you also need to listen," he said, then squeezed her arm as he pulled open the door. "I'll be inside if you need me."

Steven was making a mess out of this. He leaped up to the porch and rested his hands on either side of Katy's shoulders, but he could feel how tight she was. Being upset was something she had never been able to hide. "Hey, you, I love you," he said, "and what you heard was only a part of the story. I didn't date someone else. My parents arranged it so I was shocked, sitting there when she showed up. I didn't stay." He was trying to get her to listen as she fisted her hand, his ring still on her finger. "Katy, hear me? I left when I finally figured out what they were doing." He slid his hands over her cheeks, not wanting to see the hurt that screamed back at him.

"I told you your mom didn't like me," Katy said. "I just never expected this. Well, I don't like your mom, either. I don't want her at our wedding. How could she?" Of course she was hurt, but lashing out this way wasn't helping.

"Katy, don't do this. You can't say something like

that about my mom. What she did wasn't okay, and I'll be talking to her and to my dad. It was both of them. But they're my parents, Katy." He sighed, knowing she was still upset, and at the same time he just wanted to be alone with Katy, to reason with her. "Listen, let's go back to my place, just you and me," he said, and she flicked her gaze to him. "We can talk about things. We don't have to worry about your parents watching us and where we're sneaking off to. We can just be alone." He tilted his head, flashing her his smile, the one he knew always had her bending to him. She could never resist that.

She glanced over her shoulder and then back and nodded. "Okay," she said and pulled open the door. "Dad, Steven and I are going to go out!"

Brad must have not been far, as he was at the door and stepping out. His hands in his pockets, he took in both Katy and Steven and said, "Have fun."

Katy went into the house and ran out to Steven with her purse. "Bye, Dad," she said, and Steven took her hand. When he opened the car door for her and she slid in the passenger side, he realized as he looked back at her father that this was the first time he hadn't pressed them for more details.

The drive back to his place was done in little time. As he walked through the courtyard, holding her hand, he stopped just at the foot of the steps and looked around. This would be their place. Maybe she knew, as she slid her hand through his arm.

"Let's go, come on," she said.

He didn't let go of her hand as he led her up,

pulled his keys from his pocket, and unlocked the door. "I have a key for you," he said. "Got it cut this morning on my way over." He slipped the extra key off his keychain and stuffed it into her pocket just as he pulled her closer, sliding his hand over her butt and all her slimness. Then he had both hands touching her, pulling her closer as he backed her to the wall.

Her hands slid up and around his neck, and she linked them together as he lifted her higher. Her tongue was touching his, tasting, and he was pressing into her, lifting her tank top. She unlinked her hands so he could lift it over her head and toss it to the floor. Her skirt was already around her waist, and her pink bikini underwear were just dying to be ripped off. He was smiling as he kissed her, and she ran her hands over his shoulders, his back, holding her he turned, trying not to trip as he took her into the bedroom.

He landed with her on the bed, and she squealed, pressing her arms up. He took in her firm, high breasts. They were perky and perfect, and she never needed a bra. He was past thinking as he tasted and touched. Her legs were wrapped around his waist, and he pulled away, needing to have her naked now. He couldn't wait, didn't want to wait a minute longer as he toed off his shoes and unfastened his pants. Katy sat up and kicked off her sandals, then slid off her skirt and her underwear, dumping them on the ground. As he stood there naked in front of this beauty that would soon be his, he swore he'd died and gone to heaven, because there was no one who could walk in on them, no parents and no one listening.

Twenty

She was watching his eyes, his expression, as he moved above her. This was the first time she considered telling him to stop. She had wanted this for so long, so why was she freaking out now?

"Katy, look at me. It's okay." His voice was so gentle, and she could feel his hard length pressed against her. This was the one base they'd never gotten to before.

Maybe he knew, as he touched her lips with his lightly again and again, looking at her, whispering he loved her until she relaxed and felt her need for him finally push through her haze. It had been crazy, was all, and her emotions were all over the place, but being here with Steven was everything she'd always wanted. Just her and him and this moment. This was her first time becoming his, and she wanted more.

"I want you," she said as he moved forward, filling her tightly. She hadn't expected to feel this fullness, and then he was in, and her desire for him had dimmed. Was this what happened when girls lost their virginity?

He was moving inside her, and she wanted to tell him to stop, because it had suddenly become about him. She could feel how he was so caught up in having her that he no longer realized this was the two of them together, her first time making love. She wasn't connecting, and he was so lost in himself that the expression in his eyes, as moved inside her, was pulling away from her.

"Steven, slow down," she said. She touched his face, and he kissed her again as he moved inside her, but it was awkward for her because she didn't have a clue how this was enjoyable. She wanted to pull her legs together, but he was still inside her, and he was so big, filling her more than she could have imagined.

"Oh, baby, you feel so good. I knew you would," he said. He didn't stop as he moved faster, and Katy felt herself pushing back into the mattress, wanting to feel something but praying at the same time that it would be over. Then he yelled and swore as he moved faster.

"Steven, it hurts," she said, and he slowed just as she felt the warmth of his seed spill into her. He collapsed on top of her, still buried inside her, and all Katy could think was to ask herself what she had done.

Twenty~One

Seeing the expression on Katy's face when he finally pulled out of her was worse than being splashed with icy water. She stayed where she was, on her back, and forced a smile to her lips, one that didn't match the sadness in her eyes.

"Did I hurt you?" he asked. He'd been so caught up in being buried inside Katy and all her warmth for the first time, feeling as if he'd died and gone to heaven. He had imagined spending their weekend like this and getting out of bed only long enough to eat, but Katy wasn't smiling, and she wasn't reaching for him again. He'd pictured her sliding over him and this time riding him. They'd come close so many times, but now something had changed.

"I didn't expect it to hurt so much," she said finally and then looked away.

He slipped his hand over her cheek and rubbed his thumb over her jawline to draw her back to him. "I'm sorry. I lost my head. I promise it will be better next time," he said. He'd make sure of it. He'd go slower, make it better for her. He knew how to do that. They'd spent the last few years touching and tasting each other, and he knew how to send her over the edge.

She nodded, and he kissed her again. He started to deepen the kiss, moving to his side so he was facing her. When she slid her hand up his arm, he could hear a cell phone ringing. Katy sat up. "That's my phone," she said as she slipped off the bed.

Steven went to reach for her. "Katy, leave it. Let it go to voicemail," he said, but she was walking back into the bedroom and sat on the edge of the bed, crossing her legs as she listened.

"It was my mom. She's invited your parents to the house for dinner tonight."

"Well that's a mood killer," he said. Katy leaned on her arm and then looked down at him, at how ready he was for her again. He was positive he could make love to her all day, but at the same time he had to remind himself how rough he had been for her first time. So not cool. "I'm sorry. I should have gone slower," he said. He leaned up on his forearm, and she allowed her face to press into his hand as he touched her again. This time she gave him a smile, a little shy, but it was his Katy.

She leaned down and kissed him. "Get dressed. We have to go or your parents will be there before we are."

At least she was no longer angry, he thought as he mourned the loss of going another round with her, this time maybe letting her feel how wonderful it was. He watched as Katy pulled on her underwear and skirt and walked topless out of the bedroom to get her shirt. Maybe, just maybe, he'd be able to bring peace between his mom and Katy, and maybe his parents would accept their decision to marry and welcome her to their family.

Maybe he should just be happy his parents were at least coming over. "Small things, Steven," he said to himself as he climbed out of bed and pulled on his clothes.

"It's a pleasure to finally get together," Brad said as he shook Dez's hand, taking in the man, who was a few inches shorter than him, with heavy dark hair and a solid build.

"This is my wife, Lydia," Dez said, gesturing to her before extending a bottle of red wine.

Lydia wore a pair of jeans and a sleeveless dark turtleneck, with enough makeup and dark liner around her eyes to really make the blueness pop. Brad accepted the bottle and took in the label, a good vineyard.

Emily touched Brad's arm. "Just got a text from the kids. They're on their way back. Come in. Please sit down. Can we get you a drink?" Emily said, and Brad held up the wine.

"Why don't I open this?" he said. "Or would either of you like something else, a beer?" That was what he would have preferred, at least.

"Sure, I'll take a beer," Lydia said as she started into the living room.

"Glass of wine is good for me," Dez said, following his wife in, looking around. They took in Jack, who was sitting in a playpen, toys around him and a big grin on his face.

"So this is the little guy we've heard so much about," Lydia said. "Steven always talks about Katy's baby brother."

"Yup, our big surprise." Brad looked down on his boy, his youngest and, he had to say, the only child with whom he was taking time every day to enjoy the small moments. Maybe it was his age.

"This is a nice place, Brad, Emily. Can see why Steven likes coming over all the time," Dez said as he took a seat on the sofa, the leather swishing. "Never worried about it that much until he told us he'd asked Katy to marry him. Then, I have to say, both Lydia and I wanted to sit him down and spell out just what a stupid idea that was, especially at their age. They're kids. You both get that." Dez was gesturing to Brad and then over to Emily. Emily stepped closer to Brad, searching him out as if she hadn't expected this.

"They are young, Dez, but they're also deter-mined," Brad said. "We've talked to them, and what it comes down to is that they've decided. Bullying them and laying down the law, telling them what to think, to feel, is only going to make them run off and do something really stupid. We talked already, and they listened to a point, but their minds are already made up. You should know this, and if you keep pushing, you could alienate them. I don't want that."

Dez was sitting there with Lydia, and both of them said nothing. It wasn't so much that they were quiet, but Brad didn't know what they were thinking as he stood there, holding that bottle of wine. He heard a car, knowing it had to be Katy and Steven. Yup, he saw the flash of blue as Steven pulled in fast, the way he always did. He had to wonder, had he done the same thing at that age? Yeah, he was pretty sure he had.

"Well, there are the kids," Brad said. "We invited you here to talk about the wedding plans. We've made our peace with the kids, so I hope you're not here to try to talk them out of it. Steven told me about last night and the girl you introduced him to."

He felt Emily's gaze burn into his. He hadn't told her, of course. She looked over to Dez and Lydia and shook her head as they could hear Steven and Katy walking toward the house.

"It wasn't one of our finest moments," Lydia said. "Maybe we shouldn't have done that, but I wanted Steven to be sure the girl he settles for is the right one, because the step they're taking at their age, I seriously doubt either one of them is ready for it."

The door slapped closed. Katy was smiling, holding Steven's hand as she followed him in. Steven slipped off his shades and stuck them in his shirtfront, navy with white stripes and open at the collar. "Mom, Dad, was surprised to hear you would come after last night," Steven said. "But I was hopeful, too, that you realized you were wrong in what you did and that Katy and I are getting married." He gestured at them while holding Katy's hand. "Then I heard you just now, so I wonder if you're here to try another way. I've got to tell you that I won't let you hurt Katy. Mom, Dad, I love this girl, and we are getting married August 18. You can either be part of the wedding and accept Katy as my wife, or you won't be part of our life."

That was exactly what Brad didn't want to see happen. Hadn't he done the same thing, in a manner of speaking? It hadn't been under the same circumstances, but it had been because of anger and young arrogance.

"Steven, don't be hasty about stuff like that," Brad said. "Your mom and dad just had their chance to express their worry. So have Emily and I. You two know that. But we've said our peace. You're getting married. Your mom and dad are here tonight, and we're going to all discuss the wedding." Brad looked over to Dez and Lydia. He hoped he was right and they wouldn't keep pushing this agenda, because Katy and Steven were determined to get married, and he, for one, wasn't going to be sitting on the sidelines, cut out of their life.

It was Dez who lifted his hands and glanced to Lydia, nudging her elbow. "So August 18 is the wedding. Let's talk about who's doing the catering." When Dez glanced over to Brad, he saw a father who loved his son—and some willingness to bend.

Brad took in Katy and Steven, the way she slid

into his arms and leaned against him as she looked up. It was their moment, private, special, and he saw something so intimate pass between them: love.

Yeah, just maybe they would figure it out and surprise all of them.

"I have to go. I promised Mom and Dad I'd be home for dinner," Katy said as she settled on Steven. He was buried inside her, where he'd been for what felt like the past few hours.

She didn't think she'd ever tire of making love with him.

His hands traced lines up her back, holding her as she straddled him where he lay on the bed, his head resting on the pillow, watching her with an expression she also knew she'd never tire of seeing. She loved him more than her next breath, and he was so into her. He never tried to hide his appreciation of her body, of her.

"Not yet. You can't leave me like this," he said as she rose up and down again just a bit to tease him. She swept her fingers through her hair, lifting it as she leaned her head back.

"Okay" was all she managed to squeak out when he rolled, taking her with him so she was on her back, her legs around his waist. He looped his arms through them and held them open so she couldn't move. He was so much stronger, and she loved feeling all of his strength in moments like this.

Then he was kissing her again, a taste she thought she'd never tire of. At the same time, she felt that was all she'd done as of late: kissing Steven to the point her lips were beginning to feel bruised.

He pulled back just enough to hold himself over her on his knees, watching her as he moved faster inside her. She couldn't help it when her body took over. She reached out to him, holding his arms as she crashed over the edge that only Steven could take her to. A cry slipped from her lips. It was ecstasy, and she didn't think she could move now as she lay there. It was as if her body was becoming part of the bed.

She took a moment to catch her breath. Steven was now on top of her with all his weight, unmoving, as if he too had no strength left. She wondered whether the neighbors could hear them. She hoped not, anyway, and she was glad too that her parents had no idea what she was doing.

Or did they?

Steven pulled out and tore off his condom. "Shit, it broke," he said.

Katy couldn't help the horror as she pulled her legs together and scooted up on the bed. She took in the mess of condoms scattered in the trash and then the one that had broken. After the first time, when they'd omitted birth control, she'd been relieved to find she wasn't pregnant—but now? Although kids were on the list and the wedding was tomorrow, Katy didn't want to announce that she was pregnant too soon. She was sure that would push her mom over the edge. Brad, too.

She listened to the shower turn on in the small bathroom and knew Steven had climbed in, so she took in her clothes on the floor—shorts, a T-shirt, and a bra—as she strode to the bathroom to join him.

She touched the curtain, pulled it back, and stepped in behind him. His face was in the spray. The water was hot as she pressed against him, running her hand over his chest and lower.

"Yeah, not a good idea or I'm going to have you against the wall of this shower again," Steven said. He gripped her hand and held it away as he turned around and faced her. "It wouldn't look good for the bride to be walking oddly the day of her wedding."

She could hear a phone ringing in the background, but here was Steven, distracting her again as he smiled in appreciation, taking her in, her body, her breasts, as if he had a secret he wasn't about to share with anyone.

"That's probably Mom wondering where we are," she said, tilting her head just as Steven slipped his hand around the small of her back and pulled her closer. He nipped her neck before pressing kisses up and over her chin and claiming her lips again. She could feel how ready he was, knowing she could soon stay here all night, making love, taking time for a nap here and there but not leaving this apartment. "Just one more day, Steven," she whispered as he pulled back enough to touch his nose to hers.

Just then, there was knocking on the door. Steven looked to the side as Katy heard a voice, male, which sounded a lot like her dad. The pounding got a little louder.

"Oh no," Katy said, jumping back as Steven turned off the water. He reached for a towel, and Katy did the same, standing behind him as he dried himself off and then wrapped the towel around his waist.

He took a step out of the bathroom as the knocking sounded again. "Coming!" he said.

Katy put her hand on the door as she listened, closing it, dreading the reaction she'd see on her father's face.

Twenty-Four

"So you're Steven?" said a tall man who resembled Brad in some ways but not in others. He had more of a twang in his voice and seemed to be more of a cowboy than Brad Friessen was. His hair was lighter, not by much, and longer around the ears.

"Yeah, I'm Steven, and you are…?" He was feeling uncomfortable as he stared at all the faces he didn't recognize in the living room of Brad and Emily's ranch. There were a lot of people there, some standing, some sitting, and others mingling in the doorway of the kitchen. Relatives, he was sure, and so many kids.

"Jed Friessen, Brad's brother," the man said. He took Steven's hand, squeezed, and then slapped his shoulder as a woman with deep red hair brushed back in a ponytail stepped up beside him. She had the most brilliant blue eyes, and she smiled, carrying a toddler on her hip.

"Diana," she said and reached for Steven's hand. "You have that lost look in your eyes, seeing us all here and not a clue who we are." She was nice. He liked her. "Friessen," she added as if he was absolutely clueless. "I'm this big guy's wife." She tilted her head to Jed, the cowboy.

"Huh, well, I knew Katy had a big family. Just didn't expect all these people today," Steven said as Katy's grandfather joined them. Rodney Friessen was just a little shorter than Jed, with white hair and a kind smile.

"Good to see you again, Steven. You ready for tomorrow?" Rodney asked, but he glanced away as someone called to him. Distracted was what he seemed, what everyone seemed today. Steven didn't know where to look, whom to talk to.

"Sure," he said. Of course he was ready, considering this was all he and Katy had talked about, planned, and wanted for so long. Having Katy in his bed, waking up with her, and having no one there to walk in on them were also bonuses he'd considered.

Diana and Jed were staring at him, and even Rodney, who looked away and then back to him, seemed to hesitate. Maybe they were waiting for him to add something else.

"Steven!" Brad called out, gesturing, standing next to another potential Friessen.

"Ah, I better go and…" Yeah, not keep his future father-in-law waiting. He still felt awkward after opening his apartment door to see Brad standing there, knowing exactly what he and Katy had been doing. Brad had said not a word about it, but it was all in the look. If Steven hurt Katy, he knew the man would seriously hurt him in return.

There were kids everywhere. One grabbed his leg, a little boy playing tag with another running past. The house was hopping and seemed as if it had suddenly come alive.

"Want you to meet my cousin, Andy," Brad said.

Steven took in Andy, who also resembled Brad in some ways, but he had a hardness in his expression that made Steven a little nervous. He too was dressed casually in blue jeans and a T-shirt, with short dark hair.

"Andy, can you take the baby?" a very pretty blonde asked. She was holding a baby wearing just a diaper and a onesie. Something about Andy's expression seemed to soften as he held the infant, who had spiky dark hair and big eyes.

"Great to meet you," Steven said, looking from Andy, to the baby, to the blonde, who was smiling and running her hand up Andy's arm—another solidly built man.

"This is my wife, Laura, and our youngest, Zachary," Andy said before looking down at his wife, who was tiny compared to him. "Where are the munchkins and Sarah?" He was looking around, and Steven wasn't sure what to say as he stood there, taking in everyone talking. Someone waved from across the room. Oh yeah, Katy's grandma.

"I should go say hi to your mom," Steven said to Brad.

"Yeah, you'd better." Brad patted his shoulder. "Listen, Emily's got dinner almost ready, and your parents are on their way over."

As Brad stepped away, Steven couldn't help wondering where Katy was. He hadn't seen her yet. He made his way across the room to where Katy's grandma Becky was now sitting in a chair with her feet up, holding her grandson Jack, who held his own bottle, sucking away.

"Sit down here, Steven. Tell me how you are," Becky said. "You have to be getting excited for tomorrow."

Of course he was. It was everything he'd planned. Katy had already moved most of her things into the apartment, and the rest would come after the wedding. He still had his job apprenticing, but there'd been no word yet on whether it would be permanent. He hoped it would, but only time would tell.

"Of course," he said. "It's the big day. I know Katy and her mom planned all of it." Even his mom was helping, though, handling all the food and the catering, a big job. It was their day tomorrow, and all he had to do was get dressed, show up, and say "I do," and then Katy would be his forever. He forced a smile and then let it slide away.

"Nervous?" she asked as Jack kicked up his foot, patting the bottle and grunting.

"No, actually, I'm not. I know everyone expects us to be." He was looking around. Where was Katy?

Katy's grandma didn't say anything, as she seemed to be thinking as she watched him. "Once I was your age, young. Both Rodney and I were. The last thing any young person wants is for someone old to be telling them what to do or giving them advice they never asked for, so I'll do you a favor and keep my mouth shut, keep my opinions on what you should do to myself. But I will share this…wisdom, I'm going to call it," Becky said. "Always talk, don't get mad or think Katy should know how you feel, and never say something in anger that you can't take back, because you'll always wish you could go back to that moment and take back every hurtful thing you said to lash out at the person you love. And always say you're sorry if you've done something you shouldn't have. You do that, and you and Katy will be golden."

He thought about what she'd said. He and Katy didn't fight, not really—and when they did, he had a lot of fun making up with her.

"Oh, Steven, I wish you and Katy all the best and a very happy future together," Becky said. "Enough about that. I see you probably have met everyone." She was looking over the group and then gestured with her free hand. "Over there is Jed. He's my youngest. He and his wife, Diana, have three boys. Andy and Laura…" Becky gestured across the room from where Steven had come, and he watched as Diana handed the toddler she was carrying to Jed before heading back into the kitchen, where he could see Candy and Emily putting food out.

"Cousins, right?" he said, taking in this family of Katy's and everyone talking.

"Yes, Andy is Rodney's brother's son. He and

Laura have five children. She had the baby seven weeks ago. It's nice having all these young ones," Becky said in a proud voice.

Steven was looking to Laura and then Andy, Brad, and Jed, who were now each holding a beer, talking, laughing. He felt a hand touch his arm.

"I think your bride to be is trying to get your attention," Becky leaned in and said.

He looked up and saw Katy at the bottom of the stairs, gesturing to him. "Thanks, excuse me," he said before making his way over to her. She was wide eyed, having changed into a blue printed skirt and matching tank top.

"Hey, there you are," Steven said. "Didn't see you when I got here." He went to kiss her, but she pressed her hands to his shoulders to hold him back.

"I was getting cleaned up. Mom and Candy had some things for me to try on. That's why Dad showed up. Mom had left messages on my phone." She made a face, and Steven wasn't sure what to say. Okay, so now she was nervous, acting as if they'd just started dating and weren't getting married tomorrow. Had her dad said something to her when he insisted she ride with him back to the ranch, with Steven following?

"So…you not good?" He gestured between them, hoping he wouldn't need to go speak with Brad.

"No," she whispered loudly. "I have a problem. It's kind of a big one." She held up her phone, and he didn't know what to think.

"What is it?"

"Dad phoned again. I left him a message, and I have to call him back."

"You've lost me. What's the big deal? Call him, don't call him." He was shaking his head.

She made a face, reached for his arm, and dragged him over to the door. "The problem is that I haven't told him he's not giving me away."

He just stared down at Katy with a sick feeling, knowing Brad was planning on giving Katy away. They had all expected it to happen because Katy had promised she'd talk to her biological dad, and they'd all assumed she had. As Steven stared down at her, there was a squeak as the screen door opened and her uncle Neil stepped inside, wearing sunglasses, a case of beer over his shoulders.

"You never told your dad?" Neil said, taking in Katy and then Steven, then glancing over to Brad across the room. For the first time, Steven wanted to put his hands on Katy and shake her, but instead he groaned as he took in the look of misery on her face.

What was it about Katy and her relationship with her real dad that had her unable to speak with him?

Twenty~Five

Her uncle Neil was someone she'd always looked up to, the kind of man she could go to for anything. He was also the uncle who didn't hesitate to tell her when she'd messed up, and this time, as she stared at him as he removed his shades and tucked them in the front of his dark blue open-collar shirt, he watched her with an expression that said she'd messed up big time. Steven was rubbing his face and neck, too, looking awkwardly over to Brad, who was across the room, laughing over something Jed had said.

Maybe that was why Katy had this awful sick feeling that seemed to grow and fester. She'd kept ignoring this tiny detail she was supposed to take care of: her dad, Bob.

"I know I was supposed to say something, but I haven't seen him since my graduation night, and…" She'd chickened out after seeing how happy he had been, taking pictures of her in that amazing green gown, with Steven dressed in his dark suit beside her. She hadn't had the heart to put a damper on that evening, and every time he'd called since, her throat had clammed up when she tried to bring it up. Okay, so she was a coward when it came to Bob. She'd already admitted that to herself.

Neil was still staring at her. Steven cleared his throat.

"Katy, I need you in the kitchen," Emily said. Her mom was suddenly there, her deep brown hair brushed and hanging in soft waves down her back. She was dressed in a sheer white sleeveless blouse with a white tank top underneath. She looked lovely, and she also appeared distracted.

"Sure…" Katy started to say at the same time that Neil said, "No."

He reached over and grabbed her arm when she started to move away with her mom, and of course Emily was now frowning, looking from Neil to Katy.

"Tell your mom, Katy," Neil said.

He was going to make her face this head on, and all Katy could do was shake her head, feeling the knot that was building in her stomach grow bigger. She wanted to be ill, and she would prefer it to seeing the hurt on her mom's face, which she'd be responsible for putting there.

"Tell me what?" her mom asked. "Katy, what's going on?"

Katy looked over to Steven, who was now watching her with some understanding. He had to know the dynamics of their relationship. He'd watched from the sidelines, though she hadn't said a word to him about it. He understood, and that meant so much to Katy.

"Katy hasn't talked to Bob yet to tell him he won't be giving her away," Steven said, crossing his arms.

"Katy, what were you thinking?" Emily said, and of course she wanted to shush her mom because anyone could have heard.

"I just didn't want to bring him down, okay? I'm sorry. I'll tell him tonight, like right now. I'll call him this second," she said, staring at her phone and dreading what she had to do. When she looked up, Brad was now standing behind her mom. He was the one man, her father, that she didn't want to disappoint.

"What's going on?" he asked Emily, though he was looking down at Katy.

"I screwed up, Dad. I'm sorry..." She felt Neil's hand on her shoulder, and she just stopped talking, feeling his support and looking to him.

"Katy still needs to tell Bob he's not giving her away," Neil said. "I've said it before, Katy: I'll do it for you. I'll talk to him."

She wished he could, but he was the last person who should. Even though it would be easier, it would hurt her dad deeply, and that would turn her wonderful day into one of the worst in her life. She didn't want that, she wanted easy, but nothing about this was easy.

"No, you shouldn't talk to him. Katy, I'll talk to

your dad. I'll explain it to him so he understands," Steven said.

Well, that would be better, maybe, but she still needed to be there, to say it and explain it. She just hoped she could figure out a way for him to understand that he was still her dad, but he wasn't the father who'd raised her, cared for her, loved her, and who she relied on for everything. He had to know. Why couldn't he make this easier for her?

"No, Steven, I need to tell him. He's my dad." She squeezed her cell phone again as she took in her mom's concern for her and then Brad, the father she didn't want to disappoint. "He's just not you," Katy said as she shrugged and looked up to him. Then she looked over to Steven and lifted her phone. "Excuse me. I'm going to call Dad now."

She stepped around Neil and went outside on the empty porch, then pressed her dad's number. She heard the ring and waited for him to answer.

CHAPTER
Twenty-Six

Her head ached as she woke to the light streaming in her bedroom window, a soft breeze fluttering the curtain, moving it back and forth. Voices drifted in from outside and from other places in the house.

This was her wedding day. She should have been ecstatic, as she'd waited a lifetime for this moment, a day on which she could be a princess in a white gown in the spotlight. This was her day, and everything about it was centered on her.

Except she wasn't looking forward to it.

She had tossed and turned for hours because Bob's phone had gone to voicemail every frickin' time she'd called the night before, taking her away from the family dinner celebration. She should have been enjoying the moment and the attention, but no, she'd been glued to her phone, checking it every ten minutes to see if he'd called back. She hadn't been able to enjoy one moment with the family she loved so much.

Her dad hadn't answered, so Katy had left fifteen messages, the last one in desperation at close to midnight, saying he needed to call her before showing up for the wedding and that it was important. She stopped herself from saying he wouldn't be giving her away only because that was the kind of thing she could never leave in a message.

There was a tap on the door. "Katy, are you awake?" her grandma Becky said softly through it.

"Yeah," she croaked out. Even her throat felt dry, and it seemed an effort to talk as she sat up, reached for the second pillow beside her, and pressed it behind her back. The door opened, and her grandma stepped in. Her hair was damp, and she was wearing a blue track suit and holding a small tray with what looked like a muffin, juice, and coffee.

"Oh, looks like you didn't get much sleep," she said as she slid the tray on the bedside table and sat on the edge of the bed.

"I screwed up, Grandma." Katy pressed her hands to her face and then pulled them away. She dropped them in her lap before fisting them.

"Oh, nonsense. Is this still about your dad?" Becky reached forward and pressed her hand over Katy's.

"He's not calling me back. I called and called, and my worst fear is that he'll just show up expecting to give me away. It would be easier to just go along and let him do it…"

"Is that what you want, Katy?" Brad said. He was

leaning in the doorway. She hadn't heard him, and she felt even worse for how she was making everyone feel, especially him.

"No, it's not," she said. "You're my dad. I want you to give me away. I told you that already. It's just…"

"Oh dear," Becky said. "Sounds like you don't know how to tell Bob, but, Katy, this is your day. It's about you, not about sacrificing your happiness so you don't upset your father." Becky turned her head, and Katy wasn't sure what to make of the look that passed between her dad and her grandma. "And you probably laid awake all night?" Becky added, taking in the concern on Brad's face.

"I look that bad?" Katy asked.

"Just tired, which isn't a good thing for the bride," Becky said. "Listen, why don't you drink some coffee and juice and eat the muffin your mom made before everyone gets here and starts poking and prodding you?"

She took in her dad, who checked his watch, leaning in the doorway, dressed in jeans and a faded T-shirt.

"Don't think you'll have much time, though," he said.

She could hear cars and voices, then the door opening downstairs. "Flowers are here!" she heard her mom shout up the stairs. As her grandma handed her the steaming mug of coffee, Katy pulled up her knees. She took a swallow, and her cell phone started ringing.

She jumped and reached for it under her pillow. Seeing her dad's name on the screen, she felt relief but also regret because she knew he wouldn't take it well. "Hi, Dad," she said, taking in Brad watching her from the doorway, her grandma sitting on the side of the bed.

"Katy, something wrong? You left a lot of messages."

"Well, yeah, you didn't call me back," she said. Becky tapped her leg, stood up, and gestured that she was leaving with Brad.

"I was out," Bob said. "Didn't have a chance to call you."

What was it about him that made her always compare him to Brad? Brad would never have done that. As a matter of fact, he never *had* done that. He was always there, always available for them.

"Listen, Dad, there's something I wanted to talk to you about and should have talked to you about before now."

There was silence on the other end, and she wondered whether he already knew.

"It's about you walking me down the aisle," she said, but her voice squeaked, and she squeezed her eyes shut.

"You have no idea how much I'm looking forward to this day," Bob said. "Told all my friends. You can't imagine how excited I am to walk you down that aisle, my little girl who I raised."

He was chatting away, and she had stopped listening, as she started to feel physically sick to her stomach. It was in that moment that she realized how much easier it would have been to just elope. Then she wouldn't have had to deal with this.

"So what is it you wanted to talk about that's so important, Katy?" Bob said. "Because I'm on my way down, bringing my mom, your grandma, who's dying to spend some time with you. She's going to record the whole thing."

This was worse. She needed him to stop with all the plans. "Dad, seriously, stop. You can't give me away," she finally said.

"What? Why can't I? Of course I can. I'm your father."

She sighed and slapped her hand to the top of her head. "And so is Brad. He's my father, too. I love you, Dad, but I also love Brad, and he's giving me away." She winced as she said it, knowing it sounded awful, but she hadn't been able to figure out how to say it better.

"It's your mother," Bob said. "I knew it. She has her hands in this. She's been trying to push me out of your life since she ended our marriage—"

"Dad, stop!" she said. She was done listening to her dad do this. It had always been subtle over the years, but he'd tried to plant seeds of doubt in her head about her mom, implying Emily was somehow responsible for all of his misery.

"Katy, I'm your father. You may live there, but if you don't want me to give you away, maybe you don't want me at your wedding, either."

Of course he had taken it wrong. Why did he

always have to act like this? "Dad, that's not true. Of course I want you to come. You're not being fair. This is my choice. Mom and Dad would never insist, and they left it to me to decide, but you have to know Brad has always been there for me. He raised me, and I'm not saying this to hurt you, but you have to admit it was easier for you."

"It wasn't easier for me, Katy. Don't you think I wanted you? Because I did, but I have to work, and I don't have the money Brad does. I don't have a comfortable life, and I did the best I could. I didn't have things handed to me like your mom did."

"Dad, please, this is my wedding day. I really hope you'll come, but if this is how you're feeling, then maybe you shouldn't."

"I'm sorry you feel that way, Katy, but I'm not going to be that guy, the spectator who has to sit on the sidelines of his own daughter's wedding," he said. "Goodbye, Katy."

He hung up.

She stared at the disconnected phone, unable to believe how poorly he'd taken it. She'd never expected him to take it well, but this… She felt like crap for hurting her dad, and now she didn't know whether he'd ever speak to her again.

The entire wedding ceremony had been a blur. Steven's ring, a simple gold band, was now on her finger along with her small diamond engagement ring. She'd smiled for countless photos and stood there beside Steven, holding his hand. The bouquet of yellow lilies, carnations, and roses should have made her happy, as should the huge tent set up outside, which had been transformed with round tables, a dance floor, a stage with a band, flowers everywhere, and waiters carrying trays of drinks. It was spectacular, and all for her and Steven.

She'd also heard that the buffet, catered by Steven's parents, had been good, although the few bites she'd taken had been tasteless.

"Are you okay?" Steven asked her again. The smile she'd pasted to her face was beginning to ache.

"Of course, just tired," she said. She shrugged and looked around at everyone. Her mom and dad were dancing, her dad in a black tux, her mom in a dark blue dress with spaghetti straps. They were laughing and happy, her uncles, cousins, and family friends, and the kids were all running around. Everyone was having a great time at a wedding she'd waited forever for. She should have been talking with everyone, dancing the night away.

"No you're not," Steven said. "You're quiet and have barely said two words. You have been all day, even when your dad walked you down the aisle and kissed you and you took my hand. I couldn't figure out why you looked so unhappy, and then I realized Bob wasn't there."

She made a face as she looked up to Steven.

"What happened?" he asked.

"Dad called back, and I told him he wasn't giving me away. He started in on Mom, saying she was the reason for it and that she's responsible for his miserable life…and that he wasn't coming to my wedding." She shrugged again as she tried not to think about her mom and Brad's expressions when she told them Bob wasn't coming. She was glad they hadn't pushed it, as she found herself just getting through every moment of being pampered, her hair curled and pinned up with tiny flowers added in the bun in back. Her makeup and manicure had been a haze, as had stepping into her long white gown with a small train, full skirt, and cap sleeves that draped just off her shoulders. It was a dress she'd lost sleep over because it had made her feel like a princess the very first time she tried it on.

"This is my family. I just never expected—"

"Katy."

Her stomach dropped when she heard Bob's voice. Turning her head, she took in his short light hair, glasses, and round face. He was wearing a blue suit and a red tie and was walking toward her. Her uncle Neil was behind him, watching protectively.

"Dad, I'm glad you're here!"

He hugged her, and she slid her hands around his back and hugged him.

"You missed the wedding," she said. She was tired, and maybe that was why so many emotions were flooding through her.

"I'm sorry, you just…I never expected you to put me second like that."

She felt herself tense. "Dad, you're not second. You're still my dad, but so is Brad, and he's who raised me. That doesn't mean I love you any less." Why was she having to be the adult here?

"Glad you could come, Bob," Brad said, suddenly there, taking in her and then Bob with his deep amber eyes. He reached over and shook Bob's hand as if happy to see him. Her mom smiled, standing beside him.

"Katy was hoping you'd come," Emily added as the band struck up another song.

She noticed Brad gesture toward the stage, and then the DJ came over the microphone, saying, "We're going to have the father–daughter dance next, folks, if we can clear the floor."

She didn't know what to do, whom to dance with. She wished a giant hole would open up.

"You go dance with your dad," Brad said as he leaned in and hugged her, then kissed her cheek. "Mine's the next one."

He winked at her as he stepped back, and Katy just nodded, taking in the father who'd raised her and done everything for her as well as the other man who would always be her dad.

She stepped onto the dance floor with Bob, a man who couldn't dance but shuffled his feet back and forth, a father who fit in the background. When it came right down to it, it was Brad who would always be there for her, no matter what.

Twenty~Eight

Steven was standing in the shadows, watching as Katy, his wife of less than six hours, danced with Brad, a man who loved his family, a man Steven respected and looked up to. He hoped one day he could be the kind of man Brad was.

"There you are." It was Neil, Katy's uncle, dressed in a dark suit, a white shirt, and a deep blue tie. He was such a complex man with a head for business, always neat and tidy. Steven felt another hand on his shoulder, as well, and turned to see Jed, the other brother he'd met just the day before. He looked a little on the rougher side, wearing an older blue suit, his tie already gone and the top button of his shirt undone.

"Imagine my surprise when Bob showed up," Neil said. "Thought he'd come to his senses a little late in the day, but at least he showed. I just couldn't help myself from asking."

Steven looked over to Neil and then back to Jed,

who was watching him as if he had discovered one of his secrets.

"Asking what?" Steven said as he stared out at the dance floor, seeing Katy smiling and happy as if a weight had been lifted from her.

"I asked him what changed his mind," Neil replied.

Steven didn't say anything as he turned to Neil, knowing he knew Steven had called Bob after the ceremony, after learning from Emily that he had refused to come. Of course he knew how it had hurt Katy, and he'd considered for a moment whether she was better off not having him there. He was a man Steven couldn't respect, but he was also Katy's father, so he'd stepped away for a moment, gotten Bob on the phone, and told him how much he'd hurt Katy and that if he wanted to have a spot in Katy's future, he needed to reconsider and come to her wedding. There had been silence on the phone, and he'd worried Bob would just hang up.

"You surprise me, Steven, swallowing your pride to call a man who hurt Katy," Jed said.

His hand had been forced. What could he have said? Bob wasn't about to be the bigger person. Steven remembered what Katy's grandma had said, so he'd taken a breath and apologized for a thing he'd had no hand in, for the turn of events. Even though he'd wanted to shout at the man to grow up, he hadn't.

A hand patted his shoulder again. "Welcome to

the family, Steven," Neil said. "You may be young and foolish, but you surprised the hell out of me."

Steven tilted his head toward Katy. "She's my wife, and I love her, and that smile on her face now is worth a few minutes of groveling to a man I have no respect for. But you see that?"

Katy beamed up at Brad as he waltzed her around the dance floor, and Steven took in Bob, who was standing off to the side, speaking with a woman he didn't recognize.

"Katy is happy," he said, "and now she can look back on her special day, our wedding day, as a good memory, not one of her and her dad drifting apart. No, that day may come sometime, but it won't be today."

"Yeah, I'd say he's one of us," Jed said and laughed as he slung his arm around Steven's shoulder.

Just then, Katy glided up to him. "Come and dance with me," she said, then took his hands and pulled him onto the dance floor.

Steven lifted her arms and twirled her once, then slid his hand around her waist as he leaned down and kissed her.

Yeah, he was ready to start their lives together.

Turn the page for a sneak peek of
FAMILY FIRST from THE FRIESSENS
Available in eBook, paperback & audiobook

They never expected their happily ever after could go so wrong.

Katy and Steven never imagined that their simple dreams would come crashing around them, but six months in and this newlywed couple's carefully crafted future is crumbling. Instead of being by Steven's side, Katy finds herself with a distance between them, secrets of her own, and a divided family that could end up with Steven walking away.

SUSAN, AMAZON REVIEWER

"Wonderful read! I have loved this author and family since The Forgotten Child."

ENGLISH TEACHER

Chapter 1

The thumping above her head had finally stopped. It was so sudden that it took her a moment to realize all was quiet except for the buzzing in her ears. She was holding her breath, counting, waiting for it to start up again, but it didn't.

"Thank God, you fuckheads," she muttered, staring at a bedside clock that read two a.m. Okay, so they were early tonight. She lay there waiting, wondering whether they would decide to start up again with the loud music, the bass that vibrated the ceiling. She held her breath again, counting the seconds and waiting for footsteps, jumping, something to warn her that the insane noise was about to start up. There was nothing except the buzzing, which she put down to a ripple in the air from that godawful club music the boys upstairs continually cranked.

Then there was Steven, sound asleep, breathing even and soft with not a care in the world beside her. How in the hell could he sleep through all that?

She rolled onto her back, now wide awake. How could Steven be so oblivious as to sleep through what seemed to be a heavy metal club opening its doors in Suite 3B, the two-bedroom apartment directly above theirs? Tim and Jake were good-looking single guys, friendly enough, but they partied almost every night of the week, tunes cranked, always with a girl they brought home from the bar. As Katy lay there, wide awake, she found her outrage shifting from the upstairs tenants to Steven, who somehow always managed to sleep through the craziness.

She stared at him in the dark, her elbow now touching him. She should let him sleep. It would be the right thing to do even though she never could. No, she spent every night with a pillow crushed over her ears, awoken by the constant thudding of the worst music she'd ever heard, and she was so exhausted by lunch time that she wanted to keel over and sleep. But she couldn't, not when she was at work. Every day, as soon as she opened the apartment door and staggered in, she walked right to the bedroom and fell into bed, which was where Steven would find her when he came home from work.

She was done with that—being tired alone, that is —so she nudged Steven until she heard him stir and roll over, his arm falling over her, landing on her breast. He squeezed her as he snuggled against her.

"You awake?" He was nuzzling her neck, his hand under the sheet, running over her flat stomach and lower. She could feel him stirring and knew he'd be on top of her, her legs probably looped over his shoulders as he buried himself inside her and then fell asleep again. He was always on her, inside her, taking her everywhere and anywhere in this tiny one-bedroom apartment, right below two guys who were taking their carefree lifestyle way too seriously.

She pressed her hand to his chest and shoved when he tried to kiss her. "Okay, you need to go upstairs and have a talk with Tim and Jake. Tell them to knock it off with the music and partiers. I'm tired, and it seems they have that stereo cranked so loud the walls are shaking every single night. My ears are ringing now, and I can't sleep. I have no idea how you can. Why is no one else complaining in this godforsaken building? There are other people here, lots of people. They should be up there pounding on their door, telling them to knock it off. Why hasn't the super kicked them out?"

She couldn't believe that those two young men, although nice and friendly, hadn't been evicted. No one seemed to be doing anything about them.

Steven pulled away and was now lying on his back. He sighed, and she could tell he wasn't happy about having this conversation again. His solution to everything was to just ignore it and tell her that she was making way too much of things.

"They're quiet now," he said and gestured to the ceiling.

Jerk. She sat up, the sheet dropping to her waist as she faced him in the dark. "Just," she said. Some light streamed in the open bedroom window from the courtyard, and it was enough that she could tell he was staring at her breasts. She definitely had his attention, as his hand slid around her waist, and somehow he managed to maneuver her so she was on her back. He was settling between her legs, determined. He had a one-track mind.

"Steven, be serious…" was all she could say. He was kissing her neck, her collar bone, as he moved inside her. His hands were touching her everywhere, and she couldn't fight him anymore. One of the best parts of being married was that there were times Katy wondered who enjoyed sex more, her or him. She knew she couldn't move in bed without him touching her, and sometimes he woke her in the morning as he slid inside her.

She was lost now in just feeling Steven. Everything that had mattered moments ago faded into second place. What was it that had been so dire? She couldn't think, didn't want to think, as she moved to a place where it was only her and Steven, and the rest of the world didn't matter at all.

***

"SO WHAT TIME are you going to be home tonight?" Katy asked. She was stirring milk into her coffee. Her long blond hair, which she had yet to brush, hung tangled past her shoulders, and she appeared tired, but that did little to take away from all her loveliness. Steven loved her slender body, with curves in all the right places. He could see it all as she stood barefoot in the tiny galley kitchen in nothing more than a cotton tank and boy shorts that clung like a second skin.

"I don't know. I'll call you later." He leaned down to Katy as she walked into his arms, and he nuzzled her chin and neck. She pressed against him before running her hand over his arm. He had to step away as he realized how much he wanted her again. He cleared his throat, his jeans feeling a little tight, and Katy smiled, taking another step toward him, teasing. The minx knew exactly what she was doing as she settled her mug of coffee on the counter.

"No, you stay right there." He rested his hand on her shoulders and leaned in to kiss her, holding her back just as her arms looped around his neck. Her tongue was in his mouth, and his eyes popped open, as she somehow had her legs around his waist, pressed against him. He had to fight like a drowning man as his brain started to disintegrate, all his sound reasoning gone. All he wanted was to tear Katy's clothes away and…

His cell phone buzzed in his back pocket. He looped his arm around Katy's waist as she slid down, all the way down his front, pressing all her softness against every hard part of him. Lord, he wanted to weep as he pulled his phone from his back pocket, taking in his boss's name. Crap, his timing sucked.

"Mr. Miller." He held up his hand to Katy when she was about to touch him again. He stepped back out of her reach, mouthing "No."

"Change of plans today, Steven. Meet me at my office."

He could hear the sound of a car engine in the background. Hank must have been driving. "I haven't finished out at the Kranskis'," Steven said. "I still have to get the panel on in the pump house, then test the wires—"

Hank cut him off before he could finish. "I took care of it. Finished up early."

Of course now Steven was worrying. Had he done something wrong? "Was there a problem?" He glanced over to the clock on the stove, for a second wondering whether he was late, but it was only twenty after eight. He still had forty minutes, and he was, as always, intending on being early.

"No, your work was fine. Everything was good. Just got a call from the mister that they decided to put the house on the market. Had the realtor coming by this morning, and they wanted things wrapped up beforehand, so I was out there at dawn. Just finished up."

"Oh, okay." He still couldn't help feeling as if he'd done something, maybe because the work left to be done was his job, his responsibility, and it had been taken from him—even though it was Hank Miller's company, and, technically, it was him the Kranskis had hired. "You could have called me. I would have gone early to finish." That sounded like a whine, and for a second he wanted to take it back.

His boss sighed on the other end, and Steven realized he may have pushed it just a bit.

"I'll meet you at your house," he added quickly, trying to save face, picturing the small office Hank had built onto his bungalow. It was nothing special, but then, all the work they did wasn't in an office but in the field.

"Great, see you shortly."

He was staring at the disconnected phone, trying to make sense of the call.

"Everything okay?" Katy was standing there, holding her coffee, watching him, a question on her face. He could see it in her expression as she took a swallow from her mug, the old deep brown mugs his mom had given them.

He shook his head. "No, just a change of plans, is all. Have to meet Hank at his place. He went early and finished the job I was doing, which is odd." This was the first time Hank had done something like that, and he still couldn't shake the unease.

"Okay, well, have a good day." Katy stepped in, rising up on her tiptoes, and brushed her lips to his. Where he could have lingered before, sucked into feeling Katy, enjoying the heat in her touch, he found himself thinking, distracted. He rested his hands on her shoulders and ran his fingers over her hair to brush it behind her ears, then stepped away.

Chapter 2

As Steven drove up to Hank Miller's place and saw the older model full-size van parked in front, along with a half dozen other older vehicles that never seemed to move, he wondered who lived there with him. He knew the man was divorced. He had a daughter from his first marriage, a son from the second. On this acreage outside of town, aside from Hank's bungalow, there was also a trailer with smoke trailing from its stovepipe and a cottage that had seen better days.

An old dog wandered over to Steven as he stepped out of his blue Cavalier. "Hey there, boy," he said. The quiet dog was a mutt of some kind, a cross between a shepherd, a husky, and maybe a lab, he was pretty sure. Could be a few other mixes thrown in, as well. He patted the dog's head and could see Hank through the window of the double glass doors in the home office. He was on the phone talking to someone and didn't look Steven's way.

By the time he walked across the dirt yard, taking in the junk that seemed to be piled here and there and the many sheds in the distance, he was wondering more about the man he worked for. He tapped on the glass before opening the door and walking in.

Hank looked up and beckoned him over, then finished up his call. "Thanks, Steven, for coming out." He was sitting in an older office chair that looked as if he'd picked it up from a garage sale a decade or two ago. The wheels squeaked as he slid forward to a desk that was stacked with so much paper Steven wondered whether the man had any idea what was there. He was old school: No computer skills for this man, and organization seemed to be something he was lacking.

"Yeah, so you said the Kranskis called?"

Hank was nodding. "Yeah, they're selling. Asked for it to be finished up right away, so it's done now. I wanted to talk to you about your apprenticeship." He hadn't looked up until now, and something in his expression had Steven feeling a little ill. Steven didn't know why, but the way the man rocked a bit in the chair and cleared his throat, he seemed uncomfortable. It was making Steven sweat.

"Have I done something wrong?" His throat ached as he stared at a man he liked from across the tired old desk.

"No, no…your work is good. I'm impressed, really. When I was your age, I don't think I had the dedication you do. So get that out of your head." Hank made a face, flushed, and Steven could tell he was struggling with what he had to say. He wished he'd just spit it out. "I have to let you go," he finally said, gesturing with the flat of his hand. He looked to the side and at the desk before meeting Steven's gaze. There it was.

"I don't understand. If you're happy with my work, why?" His heart was hammering. This was the worst news, considering he and Katy had only been married six months. He had rent to pay, an apprenticeship to finish, and he was being fired!

"It's not you. I stretched it as far as I could, Steven. I haven't had any new jobs in a while. I've been giving all the work to you, hoping to pick up more, but it's the times." He rested both forearms on the desk, his shoulders hunched as he leaned forward, looking right and left as if maybe searching for more words or some divine wisdom to share. Steven, however, was doing his damnedest to understand, considering he felt as if his favorite toy had been ripped away. This was awful—worse. His happy day had suddenly turned to shit.

"So that's it?" Steven gestured in the air.

"I wish it wasn't, but the economy here… This isn't the city. If it was Olympia or Tacoma, Bellingham, even, I'd be turning jobs away, but it's not. This is Hoquiam. I've done well for a lot of years, but with eight other electricians in town, people have choices. I'm just not getting the jobs I once did." Hank opened his desk drawer and pulled out an envelope. Steven didn't have to look to know it held his last check. Even worse, the man had planned this. It must not have been sudden for him to have a check ready and waiting. Hank held the white envelope out to him as Steven stood. Obviously, this was his cue to go. This was it. Steven didn't have a clue what to do or say. It was so final.

He stood up and took the envelope, feeling the burn in his throat as he choked on all that emotion.

"I made a call to a colleague—well, to a few of them." Hank held out a scrap of paper with his scribble on it. He had about the worst penmanship, and at times Steven had to struggle to make out what the man had written. "It's something, at least. He'll finish up your apprenticeship. It's not as much money, but it'll get you done and where you need to be."

As Steven took in the phone number, he realized it wasn't local. He looked up, unable to ask, and maybe Hank understood.

"No, it's not here. It's up in Yakima. Call him, Steven. Get all your options before you say no. Again, I'm sorry. Wish I didn't have to do this."

Steven stuffed the scrap of paper in his pocket, squeezed the check, and accepted Hank's hand before stepping outside and wondering how he was going to tell Katy.

"Lorhainne Eckhart is one of my go to authors when I want a guaranteed good book. So many twists and turns, but also so much love and such a strong sense of family."

(LORA W., REVIEWER)

New York Times & USA Today bestseller Lorhainne Eckhart is best known for writing Raw Relatable Real Romance where "Morals and family are running themes." As one fan calls her, she is the "Queen of the family saga." (aherman) writing "the ups and downs of what goes on within a family but also with some suspense, angst and of course a bit of romance thrown in for good measure." Follow Lorhainne on Bookbub to receive alerts on New Releases and Sales and join her mailing list at LorhainneEckhart.com for her Monday Blog, all book news, giveaways and FREE reads. With over 120 books, audiobooks, and multiple series published and available at all, retailers now translated into six languages. She is a multiple recipient of the Readers' Favorite Award for Suspense and Romance, and lives in the Pacific Northwest on an island, is the mother of three, her oldest has autism and she is an advocate for never giving up on your dreams.

"Lorhainne Eckhart has this uncanny way of just hitting the spot every time with her books."

(CAROLINE L., REVIEWER)

The O'Connells: *The O'Connells of Livingston, Montana are not your typical family. A riveting collection of stories surrounding the ups and downs of what goes on within a family but also with some suspense, angst and of course a bit of romance thrown in for good measure. "I thought I loved the Friessens, but I absolutely adore the O'Connell's. Each and every book has different genres of stories, but the one thing in common is* *how she is able to wrap it around the family, which is the heart of each story." (C. Logue)*

The Friessens: *An emotional big family romance series, the Friessen family siblings find their relationships tested, lay their hearts on the line, and discover lasting love! "Lorhainne Eckhart is one of my go to authors when I want a guaranteed good book. So many twists and turns, but also so much love and such a strong sense of family." (Lora W., Reviewer)*

The Parker Sisters: *The Parker Sisters are a close-knit family, and like any other family they have their ups and downs. Eckhart has crafted another intense family drama… "The character development is outstanding, and the emotional investment is high…" (Aherman, Reviewer)*

The McCabe Brothers: *Join the five McCabe siblings on their journeys to the dark and dangerous side of love! An intense, exhilarating collection of romantic thrillers you won't want to miss. — "Eckhart has a new series that is definitely worth the read. The queen of the family saga started this series with a spin-off of her wildly successful Friessen*

series." From a Readers' Favorite award
—winning author and "queen of the
family saga" (Aherman)

Billy Jo McCabe Mystery: _The social
worker and the cop, an unlikely couple
drawn together on a small, secluded
Pacific Northwest island where nothing is
as it seems. Protecting the innocent comes
at a cost, and what seems to be a sleepy,
quiet town is anything but._

_Lorhainne loves to hear from her readers! You can connect with
me at:_
www.LorhainneEckhart.com
lorhainneeckhart.le@gmail.com

facebook.com/AuthorLorhainneEckhart

twitter.com/LEckhart

instagram.com/lorhainneeckhart

bookbub.com/profile/lorhainne-eckhart

pinterest.com/lorhainneeckhart

Also by Lorhainne Eckhart

The Outsider Series
The Forgotten Child (Brad and Emily)
A Baby and a Wedding *(An Outsider Series Short)*
Fallen Hero (Andy, Jed, and Diana)
The Awakening (Andy and Laura)
Secrets (Jed and Diana)
Runaway (Andy and Laura)
Overdue *(An Outsider Series Short)*
The Unexpected Storm (Neil and Candy)
The Wedding (Neil and Candy)

The Friessens: A New Beginning
The Deadline (Andy and Laura)
The Price to Love (Neil and Candy)
A Different Kind of Love (Brad and Emily)
A Vow of Love, A Friessen Family Christmas

The Friessens
The Reunion
The Bloodline (Andy & Laura)
The Promise (Diana & Jed)
The Business Plan (Neil & Candy)
The Decision (Brad & Emily)
First Love (Katy)
Family First
Leave the Light On

In the Moment
In the Family
In the Silence
In the Charm
Unexpected Consequences
It Was Always You
The First Time I Saw You
Welcome to My Arms
Welcome to Boston
I'll Always Love You
Ground Rules
A Reason to Breathe
You Are My Everything
Anything For You
The Homecoming
Stay Away From My Daughter
The Bad Boy
A Place of Our Own
The Visitor
All About Devon
Long Past Dawn
How to Heal a Heart
Keep Me In Your Heart

The O'Connells
The Neighbor
The Third Call
The Secret Husband
The Quiet Day
The Commitment
The Missing Father

The Hometown Hero
Justice
The Family Secret
The Fallen O'Connell
The Return of the O'Connells
And The She Was Gone
The Stalker
The O'Connell Family Christmas
The Girl Next Door
Broken Promises
The Gatekeeper
The Hunted

The McCabe Brothers
Don't Stop Me (Vic)
Don't Catch Me (Chase)
Don't Run From Me (Aaron)
Don't Hide From Me (Luc)
Don't Leave Me (Claudia)
Out of Time

A Billy Jo McCabe Mystery
Nothing As it Seems
Hiding in Plain Sight
The Cold Case
The Trap
Above the Law
The Stranger at the Door
The Children
The Last Stand
The Charity

The Sacrifice

The Street Fighter
Finding Home

The Wilde Brothers
The One (Joe and Margaret)
The Honeymoon, A Wilde Brothers Short
Friendly Fire (Logan and Julia)
Not Quite Married, A Wilde Brothers Short
A Matter of Trust (Ben and Carrie)
The Reckoning, A Wilde Brothers Christmas
Traded (Jake)
Unforgiven (Samuel)
The Holiday Bride

Married in Montana
His Promise
Love's Promise
A Promise of Forever

The Parker Sisters
Thrill of the Chase
The Dating Game
Play Hard to Get
What We Can't Have
Go Your Own Way
A June Wedding

Kate & Walker
One Night

Edge of Night
Last Night

Walk the Right Road Series
The Choice
Lost and Found
Merkaba
Bounty
Blown Away: The Final Chapter
He Came Back

The Saved Series
Saved
Vanished
Captured

Single Titles
Loving Christine